MUMNESIA!

Katie Dale had her first poem, 'The Fate of The School Hamster', published in the *Cadbury's Book of Children's Poetry* aged just eight and hasn't stopped writing since! Inspired by her mother, Elizabeth Dale, who is also an author, Katie loves creating characters, both on the page and onstage. After training as an actress and touring the country as Shakespeare's Juliet, she was a winner of the SCBWI Undiscovered Voices competition, which launched her writing career. She has published books for toddlers up to teens, and her novels have won several awards and are published all over the world. *Mumnesia* is her first novel for Macmillan Children's Books.

Find out more at katiedaleuk.blogspot.com

MUMNESIA!

Katie Dale

MACMILLAN CHILDREN'S BOOKS

First published 2016 by Macmillan Children's Books
an imprint of Pan Macmillan
20 New Wharf Road, London N1 9RR
Associated companies throughout the world
www.panmacmillan.com

ISBN 978-1-5098-1070-3

1 3 5 7 9 8 6 4 2

A CIP catalogue record for this book is available from
the British Library.

Printed and bound by CPI Group (UK) Ltd, Croydon CR0 4YY

For Elizabeth Dale – my wonderful mum
and my best friend x

SUNDAY

1 LUCY

OMG, it's official. Sharon hates me. Why else would she ruin my life?

'Lucy, I said no.' Her frazzled bun bobs as she shakes her head.

'But, Sharon,' I cry, jumping up from the kitchen table, 'that's so unfair!'

'No, it's not.' She glares at me as she fills the sink with steaming water. 'And don't call me Sharon. I'm your mother.'

'Allegedly,' I mutter, slumping in my seat and scowling at her as I stab at the remains of my tasteless tofu stew. Honestly, we're so unalike I swear the only thing I've inherited from her is my mousy-brown hair – and I hate my hair! Why, of all the girls in my year, do I have to be the one with an uber-uptight control-freak mum? Who thinks sunset means bedtime, make-up and chocolate are mortal sins, and a monthly book club is a social life? #AsIf

'Please, *Mum* –' I clear the table and sidle up to her as she starts the washing up – '*everyone* else is going. Even Kimmy!'

1

Mum raises an eyebrow. '*Even* Kimmy? I thought she was your best friend?'

'She is,' I grumble, scraping the scraps into the bin. 'When she has time. Which is *never*.'

'Don't exaggerate.'

'I'm not!' I protest, dumping the dirty dishes on to the counter with a clatter. 'She's suddenly become this mahoosive fitness freak – playing boring sports before, after and even *during* school, leaving me by myself like Billy-no-mates!' I hug my arms tightly.

'Well, just make some new friends,' Mum says, stacking clean plates on the draining board.

'I'm trying!' Like it's that easy! 'But if I don't go to the ball, it'll be impossible! I'll be left out of every conversation for the rest of term!'

'Don't be such a drama queen!'

I grit my teeth. Why doesn't she ever take me seriously?

'Maybe you should take up a sport too,' she suggests. 'You could do with getting a bit more exercise.'

'Like dancing?' I suggest, batting my eyelashes. 'At a ball?'

'No!' Mum snaps. 'Now, please, give it a rest, Lucy. I've got a headache.'

'So we can't even *talk* about it?'

'We have talked about it.' She grips the washing-up brush so tightly I think it might snap. 'I said *no*.'

Like that's fair.

I shove a slice of bread into the toaster and yank the handle down roughly. She just doesn't get it. The Black and White Ball is a BIG DEAL. It's all everyone at school's been talking about for weeks, plus it's possible – just possible – that Zak will be there. #Swoon

Just the thought of him cheers me up – his gorgeous floppy black hair, his melted-chocolate eyes, that lovely lopsided grin . . . Not that he's ever smiled directly at me. Or even *looked* at me actually, but every day I watch out for him in assembly, hoping that our eyes will finally meet, that I'll actually get up the guts to talk to him.

But at a ball . . .

I can just imagine it. A disco ball sprinkling everyone with swirling glittering lights, as a slow song comes on, our eyes meet across the dance floor, he smiles, and—

Pop! My toast jumps up, startling me from my daydream. I cover it in thick, gooey chocolate spread – perfect comfort food – but just as I'm about to take a bite, Mum snatches it off me with her wet soapy hand. Gross!

'No sugar before bed,' she chides, dropping it into the bin.

'But, Mum!'

'And stop sulking,' she says. 'It'll give you wrinkles.'

Like she can talk! But pointing out that she's got

hundreds of wrinkles probably won't help my case . . .

I take a deep breath. 'Can I at least ask *why* I can't go to the ball?'

She looks away. 'Well, for one thing you're too young.'

'It's a *school* ball!' I cry. '*At school*. For schoolchildren. How on earth can I be too YOUNG?!'

'Lucy,' she says, wincing.

'Sorry!' I'd forgotten about her headache. Time for a new approach. I pick up a tea towel. 'Here, let me help.'

'Thank you. But you still can't go, Lucy. It's my weekend with you. I've made dinner plans,' Mum says, handing me some wet cutlery.

'We have dinner together every day!' I protest. 'We just *ate* dinner together! Can't we rearrange it?'

'No.'

'Why not? You're so unreasonable!' I moan, shoving the cutlery into a drawer and slamming it shut – forgetting it has one of those 'soft-close' mechanisms. #Fail

'No, you're extremely ungrateful!' Mum scolds, violently scrubbing a baking tray.

'I'm not!' I insist. 'I'm happy to go out to dinner – I'm happy to *pay* for dinner on *any other day*! I'll pay for my ball ticket too!'

'Oh really? With what?'

'I'll . . . get a Saturday job,' I say.

'Oh, Pumpkin, you're only twelve years old.' Mum smiles sympathetically as she picks up a saucepan. 'You're too young to get a job.'

'Then I'll ask Dad for an advance on my pocket money.'

'You will not!' The pan clatters into the sink, splashing suds everywhere.

'He won't mind!' I argue. 'He told me if I ever need money just to ask, so—'

'I said NO!'

OK, so maybe mentioning Dad wasn't such a great idea. I overheard them arguing on the phone earlier and Mum's been uber-touchy ever since. Which is weird, as they've never argued much – even when they were getting divorced. Not in front of me anyway. Don't get me wrong, I was completely gutted when they split up – and devastated when Dad moved in with his blonde Aussie fitness-freak girlfriend, Irritating Ingrid – but now . . . Dad seems younger somehow; he's out meeting new people, having fun – while Mum just seems more stressed. I glance over at her, her grey roots showing more every day, and I'm not sure which one looks more tired, Mum or the shapeless baggy dress she's wearing. I swear it's older than me, repaired to within an inch of its life, like everything in her wardrobe. #FiftyShadesOfBeige. She could do with some new clothes. She could do with some fun. Like going to a *ball*, for instance . . .

'Why don't you come to the ball too? They need chaperones,' I suggest. 'That way we could still spend the evening together?'

'You must be desperate.' Mum raises an eyebrow. 'I thought I embarrassed you?'

'Of course not!' I lie awkwardly. But having my embarrassing mum there would be better than not going at all. *Just*.

'What's the big deal anyway, Lucy?' Mum asks. 'Why are you so keen to go to this ball?'

Zak's dreamy face dances in my mind.

'Well . . . it's just . . .'

'Wait!' Mum says suddenly. 'Is this about a *boy*?'

My heart lifts. She *does* understand! 'Yes! Oh, Mum, he's so—'

'I *knew* it!' she cries, throwing her hands up and flicking grotty washing-up water all over me. 'Pumpkin, you're too young to have a boyfriend.'

My heart plummets. 'But you met Dad when you were my age!' #Hypocrite

'That was completely different.'

'How?' I demand.

'We were just friends at your age! We didn't start dating till we were much, much older. And neither will you. Boys are too distracting.'

'But Zak could *help* me with my schoolwork!' I insist.

6

'He came top in the maths challenge and—'

'Wait, Zak *Patel*?' Mum turns. 'Nina's son?'

'Um . . .'

'Lucy!' Mum's eyebrows shoot up. 'He's two years older than you!'

'So? Dad's *ten* years older than Ingrid!' I retort before I can stop myself. #UberHypocrite

'I'm aware of that,' Mum says quietly. 'But he's a grown-up. Allegedly.' She brushes a hair from my face with her soapy fingers. 'And you're my little Pumpkin.'

'I'm not a freaking *pumpkin*!' I protest, flinging down the tea towel, my blood boiling. 'I'm not a child any more, but you can't even see it!'

'You'll grow up soon enough, Lucy.'

'How?' I exclaim. 'How am I *ever* supposed to grow up if you won't *let* me?! All my school friends get space and independence and phones and freedom – but not me! It's so unfair, Sharon!'

'I've told you, don't call me that!' she snaps. 'I'm your mother!'

'No, you're my *dictator*!'

'Lucy, this conversation is over! Go to your room.'

'See?' I yell. 'Dictator!'

2 SHARON

It's official. Lucy hates me. She slams the kitchen door behind her, making the cups on the draining board rattle and my head pound painfully. Terrific.

I finish washing up, put the leftover stew in a tub in the fridge, then decide to get an early night – anything to get rid of this splitting headache. I pause outside Lucy's room, hoping she's still up, but she's snoring gently. I trudge to my own room, my heart heavy. I hate going to bed without resolving an argument. I wish I could just be honest with Lucy, about Saturday night, about her dad, about *everything*. Then maybe she wouldn't think I'm such a tyrant. But I guess it's a mother's job to be the bad guy now and then.

Sometimes I really hate being the grown-up.

3 LUCY

I lie still, eyes shut, pretending to snore until she goes away.

#Grrr

I hate her. And I hate being a kid! Life is so much simpler for grown-ups – they can do *whatever* they want, *whenever* they want – not to mention get to completely and utterly dictate their kids' lives.

Doesn't she see how hard it is being nearly thirteen? Doesn't she *care*?

I wish, just for a day, she could remember what it's like being twelve.

MONDAY

4 SHARON

My eyes fly open, my heart racing a mile a minute, sweat sticky on the back of my neck, my duvet over my head.

I take a deep breath and try to calm down.

I must've had a nightmare – a terrible nightmare – but what about?

I can't even remember . . .

Whatever it was, it was just a dream, I remind myself. It wasn't real, and I'm safe in my own bed . . . But as I reach for my pillow, I realize it's not! *My* pillow's pink, but this one's brown! Bizarro. Where's it come from? And where's mine . . . ?

I yank the duvet off my head, and my jaw drops.

Holy guacamole! WHERE ON EARTH AM I?

Where's my pink bed and dressing table? Where are my posters and keyboard? I gaze at the HUGE bed, pine furniture and white walls, goosebumps prickling my arms.

Where am I? How did I get here? WHAT'S HAPPENED? My heart beats loudly, making it impossible to think, to remember . . .

Have I been *kidnapped*? Oh my giddy aunt, THAT'S THE ONLY POSSIBLE EXPLANATION!

Deep breaths, take deep breaths, I tell myself, trying desperately not to scream. What would Nancy Drew do?

Escape!

To my surprise, the door isn't locked. I peek outside and see a long white hallway, with several other doors and a window, but they're all closed. I hold my breath and tiptoe carefully out.

Then suddenly I hear a toilet flush and one of the other doors opens!

I freeze.

What should I do? Run? Hide? Find something to hit the kidnapper with? I grab the first thing I see – an orchid in a pot from the windowsill. Terrific.

I clutch it tightly, ready to defend myself. But to my surprise a girl in school uniform hurries out. She must've been kidnapped too!

'Psst!' I hiss.

She spins around, startled. 'You scared me!'

'Shh!' I whisper, grabbing her hand. 'Come on!' I drag her quickly along the corridor.

'What the . . . ? What's going on? Why are we whispering? Wait – *Is there someone here?*' Her eyes widen as she stops dead. 'OMG!'

OMG? Is that our kidnapper? I try to think of anyone

11

I know with those initials . . .

'Sharon!' she gasps, pulling her hand free.

I stare at her. 'You *know* me?'

'Well, I'm not so sure any more!' she exclaims, putting her hand on her hip. 'How did this happen? *When* did it happen? After I went to bed? And what's with the plant?'

'SHH!' I hiss nervously. 'Let's just get out of here!' I grab her arm but she doesn't budge.

'We can't just *leave*!' she protests.

'*Why not?*'

'Well, you're in your *nightie*, for a start!'

'*So?*' I hiss. This is totally not the time to worry about *fashion*!

She folds her arms. 'Look, just tell him it's time to go.'

My jaw drops. She wants me to *find* the kidnapper and say we're *leaving*? Nancy Drew never did anything like that!

'I . . . I can't!' I squeak.

'Fine. I'll do it then! This is ridiculous!' She knocks loudly on the door of the room I woke up in. 'Hello?'

'There's no one in there,' I whisper.

She frowns, then marches boldly down the corridor, sticking her head in through every doorway. 'Hello? Is there anybody there?'

I hover behind her, orchid at the ready.

'Hello?' She calls. 'Hello, hello, hello! There's no one here, Sharon.'

'What about this room?' I point to the one door she hasn't checked.

'He'd *better* not be in there!' the girl growls, storming inside. 'Nope. Coast's clear!'

'Thank goodness!' I breathe a sigh of relief as I follow her – and then my eyes nearly pop out of my head! Unlike the pristine hallway and the room I woke up in, this bedroom is majorly cluttered, with stuff spilling over every surface – *but what crazy stuff*! A bookshelf is overflowing with what look like impossibly flat, plastic books – except one's lying open and there aren't any pages, just a doughnut-shaped hole . . . bizarro! Then there's a huge, wide, ridiculously thin screen attached to the wall, and – wait – something just moved on the bedside table. My eyes flick to the picture frame. Weird – I swear it was a different photo a moment ago . . . Oh my giddy aunt, it just changed *again*! What is going on? Is O.M.G. a spy? An alien? Have we been kidnapped by *alien spies*?

'Holy guacamole!' I gasp. 'Look at this place!'

'Don't start,' the girl grumbles. 'My room, my mess. If you don't like it, don't come in.'

'*Your* room?' Wait. She *lives* here?

She rolls her eyes. 'OK. Technically it's *your* house,

so it's *your* room. Satisfied?'

'*What?*' Now I'm majorly confused. *My* house? I gaze around at all the strange machines and contraptions, my head spinning. Where am I? How did I get here? How does this girl know me? *And why can't I remember?*

Then my eyes fall on a calendar. And I scream.

5 LUCY

'*What's happened?* What's wrong?!' My heart beats fast as I spin round to find Mum's favourite plant pot smashed at her feet, orchid and wood chips strewn all over the carpet.

'Is . . . is this a joke?' she stammers, her face deathly pale as she pulls my calendar off the wall. 'What . . . what's the date?'

'Monday the . . . I dunno, fourteenth of October? You've got the calendar.'

'So this . . . this is *this year's* calendar?' Mum thrusts it under my nose.

'Er, yes,' I say, taking it. 'Why would I have a calendar for any other year?' #Weird. And why isn't she at all bothered about the broken pot? #UberWeird

'Oh my giddy, giddy aunt!' Her hands fly to her cheeks. 'How has this *happened*?'

'What? What's happened?' I scan the calendar anxiously, but there's not even anything marked on it for today. 'Have we missed something important?'

'Only about thirty years!' Mum's face crumples. She looks as if she's on the verge of tears.

'*What?*' Fear flutters in my stomach. 'What are you *talking* about?'

'You won't believe me.' She shakes her head. '*I* don't

believe me. Oh my goodness, how did I *get* here? And why *here*? Why *now*?'

A cold shiver runs down my spine as I watch my always-calm, always-in-control mother lurch wildly around my room, staring at my stuff as if she's never seen any of it before. 'Look, just . . . just calm down, OK?' I beg. 'You're starting to freak me out!'

'*I'm* freaking out!' she squeals.

'But *why*?'

'Because I – I must've TRAVELLED THROUGH TIME!'

She looks at me, her eyes wild and confused, then suddenly bursts out laughing.

'Is . . . is this a joke?' I say uncertainly. 'Because I don't get it.'

'No!' She insists. 'It's not a joke! Yesterday when I went to bed it was 1985, and now . . . I'm in the FUTURE! This is AWESOME!' She gazes round the room. 'Is that a *television*? It's enormous!'

#OMG. She's finally flipped.

'And what's this?' She picks up a DVD case from the floor. '*X-Men* . . .'

'Um, I have no idea how that got here,' I lie automatically. 'Kimmy must've lent me the wrong movie. By accident.'

'It's a *movie*?' Her eyes widen as she pops the disc out. 'Cool!'

'*Cool*?' My heart pounds in my ears. Mum absolutely *hates* superhero films – she says they're mindless violent fantasies. 'Who are you and what've you done with my mother?'

'I'm so sorry!' she cries. 'I thought you knew – I'm Sharon Miller, nice to meet you.' She shakes my hand. 'But I don't know where your mother is. Sorry – I just got here.'

What? My mind feels like it's about to explode. Is she having a nervous breakdown? What should I *do*?

She gazes intently at the DVD. '*Totally* space age. Can I take one back with me?'

'Back?'

'Yeah. I mean, if I can take stuff – I don't know how time travel works!' She laughs. 'My science teacher said we couldn't – or was it shouldn't? – travel through time, because of the danger of creating rifts in the space–time thingummyjiggy – so he'd totally flip out if I brought this into school!'

'*School*?' I stare at my middle-aged mother. 'How *old* are you?'

She straightens her shoulders. 'Twelve.'

My eyebrows shoot upward. '*Twelve*?'

She nods. 'Why? How old are you?'

17

Suddenly all my panic turns to rage. 'Oh, I *get* it. This is all some kind of twisted role play to show me how immature I am? Nice one, Mum. Funny. Not!' I snatch the DVD off her and shove it into my school bag, my cheeks burning. I can't believe I *fell* for that!

'Wait,' she says quietly. 'You're my . . . my *daughter*?'

'According to my birth certificate.' I scowl, yanking the zip closed.

'Oh my . . .'

Something in her voice makes me turn.

'For real?' she says, all colour draining from her face.

My heart skips. If she's acting, she deserves a flipping Oscar.

'Mum, seriously . . .' I swallow hard, and my voice is barely a whisper when I say, 'Are you OK?'

'No!' She shakes her head frantically. 'I'm not supposed to travel within my own timeline! What about the space–time thingummyjiggy?'

OMG, she really, truly, thinks she's *time-travelled*? I bite my lip. Is that even *possible* . . . ? I try to remember what we learned in physics – if only I'd paid more attention!

'I mean, of all places to time-travel to – of all the people to meet!' Mum clasps my hand. 'I can't believe you're my *daughter*! But how did you *recognize* me?'

My jaw drops.

'Of course – you must've seen old photos!' She smiles suddenly. 'Dad's always got his Polaroid camera out. It's, like, *so* embarrassing.'

'Um . . . it's not from photos,' I say slowly.

She frowns. 'Then how?'

I take a deep breath, then lead her to my wardrobe – with its full-length mirror . . .

6 SHARON

A blood-curdling scream rips from my throat. 'What's *happened* to me?' I back away from the mirror in horror. 'I'm OLD! *Majorly* old! Like, at least twenty-five!'

The girl snorts. 'And the rest!'

'I . . . I must've somehow transported into the body of my future self!' I frown at my ancient reflection, then gasp in disgust as my forehead creases into a million lines. 'Gross! I've got *wrinkles*!' I wail, trying to smooth them out with my fingers. 'And *grey roots*!'

The girl nods. 'I've been telling you to dye them for ages.'

'Why didn't I?'

'It's like you stopped caring ever since D—' She stops suddenly.

'Since what?'

'Since you dyed it the first time,' she says quickly.

I shake my head, still struggling to take it all in. I can't believe just yesterday I was twelve years old, totally flat-chested, praying for my spots to clear up, and now . . . well, now I've got boobs at least, and the spots are gone — but there are big bags under my eyes, wrinkles everywhere, and — ugh! — saggy skin beneath my chin. I prod it — and it wobbles! *Gross!*

'This is so freaky,' I squeal. 'Like that movie – *Freaky Friday*!'

'Yeah.' The girl nods. 'Except unlike Lindsay Lohan, I haven't changed too, thank goodness!'

'Who?' I ask.

'Lindsay Lohan,' she repeats. 'The daughter.'

'You mean Jodie Foster!'

'Who?' She frowns, twirling a strand of hair around her finger – just like I do – and suddenly I can't help but smile. She's my future *daughter*. How incredible is that? It's even more unbelievable than travelling through time!

'So, like, what's your name?' I ask shyly. It seems like a crazy question to ask my own daughter, but . . . 'Wait!' I snap my fingers. 'Lucy?'

She stares at me. Then nods. Then her eyes narrow. 'Is this all fake, Mum?'

'No!' I insist. 'I promise!'

'Then how would you know—'

'It's my favourite girl's name,' I explain. 'Ever since I read *The Lion, the Witch and the Wardrobe*.'

Lucy smiles nervously and sits down on the bed. 'That's my favourite book.'

'Me too!' I cry, plonking myself down next to her. 'And, please, call me Shazza. Mum sounds so *old*!'

'*Shazza?*' she splutters.

21

I nod. 'That's what my friends call me. I *hate* the name Sharon!'

'OK . . . Pleased to meet you . . . Shazza.' Lucy smiles shyly.

'Pleased to meet you too, Lucy.' I beam.

7 LUCY

'I can't believe we're both twelve!' Shazza cries, grabbing my hands excitedly. *'That's so weird!'*

'This is *all* uber-weird!' I cry, staring at her as she jumps up to peer at the mirror again, as if gazing at a stranger. But it's also pretty cool. I mean *time travel*? Wow!

'Hey, look at my ears – they're *pierced*!' Shazza squeals. 'Rad! Wonder when that happened. I've been begging Ma for *ages* but she always says I'm too young.'

'Tell me about it,' I mutter.

'Yours won't let you either?'

'Uh, *you* won't, no.'

She blinks. 'Right. Me.' She frowns. 'Future-me.'

'But *you'd* let me, wouldn't you?' I say quickly.

'What?'

A slow smile spreads across my face. *'You'd* let me get my ears pierced, right, Shazza?' I am overwhelmed by the geniusness of my plan – now I'll definitely know if she's putting on an act!

She looks conflicted for a moment and I'm almost sure I've called her bluff . . . but then she shrugs. 'Why not?'

'Why not?' I stare at her. 'Seriously?' I'm torn between being uber-thrilled and uber-freaked out.

'Come on!' She grabs my hand. 'Let's do it!'

OK, so freaked out beats thrilled. By a landslide. Especially when she asks me to fetch a needle and two ice cubes and says we should go into the bathroom 'in case it gets messy'.

Messy how . . . ?

'Relax!' Shazza laughs as I perch on the side of the cold bathtub. 'Stop shaking – I don't want to stab you in the face!'

Funnily enough, this does not help me relax. 'Um, have you done this before?' I ask nervously as she squeezes my earlobe between the ice cubes.

'Yep. Just last night actually.'

'*Last night?*'

'I mean – well, decades ago, I guess!' She giggles. 'I pierced my friend Kelly's ears. Well, ear.'

'She only had one done? Is that an eighties thing?'

'Well, no, she was going to have both, but she fainted after the first one. Lame.'

'She *fainted*?' I gasp.

'Kelly always freaks out at the sight of blood.'

My stomach lurches. '*Blood?*'

'It was the same in biology when we dissected hearts,' Shazza says, squinting with concentration as she lifts the needle to my very-cold-but-nowhere-near-numb-yet earlobe. 'Now, just hold still—'

'Wait!' I cry, jumping up out of her reach.

'What's the matter?'

'I . . . er . . .' I search desperately for an excuse.

'Have you changed your mind?' she asks, the needle still glinting in her hand.

'I . . .' *Hang on* – is that her *plan*? Is she trying to scare me off getting my ears pierced? Is she really still Mum? *Who's* bluffing *who* here . . . ?

'It'll only take a minute!' She smiles encouragingly.

'Is that the time? I've gotta go!' I'm not taking any chances where needles are involved!

'Go where?' She frowns.

'Duh! School!'

'*School?!*' Shazza grabs my arm. 'No, no, no! You can't *leave* me! Take the day off!'

#JawDrop. 'You mean . . . *skip school*?'

'Yes!' she cries. 'Say you're ill! Stay home! *Please*, Lucy!'

'Wow.' I sink on to the toilet lid, dizzy with shock, all my doubts instantly skittering out the window. 'Mum – the old Mum – would never in a *million years* let me bunk off. My school had to send *me* home when I had chickenpox!' I look up. 'You're really not her, are you?'

She shakes her head. 'Not yet!'

'But . . . *how did this happen*?'

'I've no idea!' Shazza shrugs.

'I mean, do you have a . . . a *time machine* or something?' I ask.

'No.'

'And how did you end up in Mum's middle-aged body?'

'I don't know!' Shazza insists. 'All I know is, yesterday I was twelve years old in 1985, and now I'm here, like this! I wish I knew how. I wish I knew why.'

#LightBulb! *'That's it!'* I cry, jumping up. 'It's my *wish*!'

'What?'

'Last night I *wished* that Mum – Old Mum – knew what it was like to be twelve for a day, and now you're here: twelve-year-old Mum!'

Shazza stares at me. 'You *wished* me here?'

'I know it sounds crazy, but—'

'No – it all makes sense!' She beams, hugging me tight. 'Wow . . . so *that's* why I travelled through time! That's totally AMAZING! Plus, if I'm only here because of you, and I'm only here for ONE DAY, you're *definitely* skipping school!'

'Deal!' I laugh. And for once I'm actually glad Kimmy has sports practice on Monday mornings instead of walking to school with me; this would take a *lot* of explaining!

We hurry into the lounge and Shazza bounces on the

sofa as I ring the school then pass her the phone.

'Oh *hello*!' she trills as the secretary answers, and I have to bury my face in a cushion to muffle my giggles. 'I just wanted to let you know my daughter can't come to school today. Lucy Miller.'

'Andrews!' I hiss urgently. 'Lucy *Andrews*!'

'I mean Andrews! Sorry! Miller's my maiden name,' Shazza says quickly, then covers the mouthpiece, her eyes sparkling. 'Andrews? Really?' she whispers. 'Who did I *marry*?'

'Shh!' I hiss, pointing at the phone.

'Sorry, what? Oh, she's ill. No, nothing infectious, just um . . .' Shazza hesitates. 'She's got . . .'

'Flu! Tonsillitis! Food poisoning! Anything!' I mouth, but she still looks stumped! Exasperated, I flap my arms to mime 'flew'.

'The doctors think it's . . . um . . . chicken—' Shazza begins.

'*Flu!*' I hiss. The school knows I had chickenpox last year – and you can't have it twice! Plus it'll look well suss when I go back to school tomorrow, pox-free.

'Flu.' Shazza finishes, giving me a thumbs-up. 'That's right. Chicken flu. No, I'd never heard of it before either.'

I roll my eyes. *Chicken flu?*

'Is it like what? Bird flu?' Shazza looks at me blankly. I shake my head wildly. OMG, she'll start a mass panic!

'No, no, it's more like normal flu – but you get it from eating chicken,' she says triumphantly. 'You know, like salmonella.'

#Facepalm

'Gotta go – bye!' Shazza hangs up quickly.

'*Chicken flu?!*' I exclaim, throwing my cushion at her.

'I'm sorry!' she wails. 'I thought you were pretending to be a chicken! But more importantly, if *I'm* MRS ANDREWS, then *who* is MR ANDREWS?' She bounces up and down, hugging the cushion. 'Holy guacamole, this is going to save so much heartache! Now I won't have to waste my time dating loads of losers cos I know it won't work out!'

I bite my lip. Should I tell her that it doesn't exactly work out with Dad either? But she looks so happy, and she's only here for one day . . . Why burst her bubble?

'Of course, dating is totally fun, so I might go out with other boys anyway!' Shazza continues.

'*What?*' I cry. 'You're *dating*?'

'Of course!' She laughs.

Unbelievable. Yet *I'm* not allowed? #Hypocrite!

'But Trev is by far the coolest guy I've dated.' Shazza beams. 'We've been going out for three weeks now. I sneak out my bedroom window to meet him when Ma and Pa think I'm doing my homework.'

'You do not!' I gasp.

'Do so. Out the window, down the apple tree. Easy peasy, lemon squeezy.'

OMG, I am going to have SO much ammo against Mum when she changes back!

'But I guess it doesn't work out.' Shazza slumps back on the sofa. 'Trev's surname's Lawrence, not Andrews.'

'Yeah, and Dad's called Daniel.'

'Daniel Andrews . . . ?' Shazza's eyes widen. 'Wait, *Danny* Andrews?'

I shrug.

'Holy guacamole!' Shazza squeals. 'It can't be the same Danny Andrews – that's just too *bizarro*!'

'Um . . . why?'

'Detective Dan's a friend at school!'

Detective Dan?

'Show me a picture! Quick!' She jumps up. 'I need to know if it's the same guy!'

'Um, we've got digital cameras these days so we don't really print photos much—'

'What about the magic photo frame by your bed?'

'Er, there aren't any pictures of Dad on it,' I fib.

'Come on, there must at least be a wedding album or *something*!' Shazza begs, pulling me to my feet. 'Show me, show me, *show me*!'

I hesitate. But what harm can it do? 'I think there's

one on top of Mum's wardrobe – I'll get it.'

But Shazza is already racing down the corridor whooping.

#UhOh

8 SHAZZA

'I can't believe I'm going to see my wedding photos!' I cry, bouncing up and down on Sharon's enormous bed as Lucy stands on a chair, rummaging through the stuff on top of the wardrobe. 'This is so exciting!'

'Look at you!' Lucy laughs as she opens a box. 'You *never* let me jump on my bed!'

'Really? But it's, like, majorly fun! Oh my giddy aunt, *is that it*?' I squeal as she pulls out a big white book. 'Lucy, IS THAT MY WEDDING ALBUM?'

'Yes,' she says, smiling.

'HOLY GUACAMOLE!' I take it from her carefully and sit down with it on my lap. I trace my fingers over the flowers and bells and silver swirly writing on the creamy cover, and I tingle with excitement. And nerves.

'What's wrong?' Lucy asks, flopping down beside me.

'Suddenly everything my science teacher said about not travelling within your own space—time thingummyjiggy is ringing in my ears!' I wail. 'Should I really do this? It's going to have, like, major spoilers, and once I see them I can't ever *un*see them . . .'

Lucy laughs. 'Shazza, the space—time thingummyjiggy is already pretty busted. You're in your future house with your future daughter and you know who your future husband is. I really don't think looking at a few wedding photos is going to make any difference, do you?'

She's totally right. I take a deep breath, my stomach fluttering with a million butterflies as I slowly open the cover . . .

'Holy guacamole, I look like a princess!' I gasp, gazing at the beautiful puffy dress, the long lacy train and my enormous smile. I look so happy and so much younger than now – I had hardly any wrinkles. 'Did I get married in a castle too?'

'Um, no, I think it was a registry office?'

My heart plummets. 'Really?'

'But it was really beautifully decorated – look!' Lucy turns the pages quickly, but I stop her when she reaches a picture of the groom.

'Oh my giddy, giddy aunt, it *IS* Danny!' I peer closer. 'But what happened to his mullet?'

'*What?*' Lucy shrieks. 'I can't even *imagine* Dad with long hair!'

'I can't wait to see what he looks like now!' I grin, closing the album and hugging it excitedly. 'Where is he anyway? At work?'

Lucy nods slowly, a strange look flickering across her face.

'So he'll be back around, like, five-ish? Six-ish?'

'Actually . . .' Lucy says slowly, 'he's away. On a business trip.'

'Wow!' I cry. 'How exciting! What does he do? Wait, is he a detective? He always *dreamed* of being a detective!'

'Er . . . no, he's an accountant.' Lucy gets up quickly and shoves the wedding album back on top of the wardrobe.

'Ugh! Boring!' I grimace. 'I suppose it could be worse. He could be a traffic warden or something. Wait, what do *I* do?' I ask anxiously, twirling my hair.

'You're . . . a traffic warden!' Lucy laughs.

'WHAT?' I flop backwards on the bed in horror. 'I can't be! Please, please, *PLEASE* tell me you're kidding!'

'I am.' Lucy giggles, grabbing my hands and pulling me back upright. 'You're a librarian.'

'What? No way!' I say, surprised. 'Bizarro. Though I do majorly love books. I always dreamed of being an author one day.'

'Really?' Lucy smiles, sitting next to me. 'I never knew that.'

'I've never told anyone before,' I admit shyly. 'It's so strange. Even though we've only just met, somehow I feel like I can tell you anything. I guess it's a mother–daughter thing.' I hug my knees, a warm feeling flooding through me. 'Do we tell each other all our secrets?'

Lucy hesitates. 'Not exactly,' she mutters, fiddling with her hair.

33

'That's a shame. But I guess I don't tell Ma everything either! If she knew how often I bunk off school, she'd probably kill me!'

Lucy's eyes widen. '*You* bunk off *school*?'

'Doesn't everyone?'

'No!' She gasps. 'You'd ground me for life!'

'Wow.' I wince. 'I'm majorly strict, huh? Weird. Well, not today! Today we are gonna have FUN!'

9 LUCY

Listening to Shazza call in sick has got to be in my all-time top ten moments ever!

'I'm – *sniff* – really sorry but – *cough cough* – I just don't think I'll be able to – *sniff* – make it in today – *aaaatishoo!*' she says in a really pathetic voice. 'Ever since I woke up I just feel really – *cough cough* – weak and – *sniff* – like I'm totally about to be . . . um . . . *Bleurgh!*' She runs to the kitchen sink and yanks the tap on and off as she makes a noise like she's throwing up and I have to clap my hand over my mouth to stop myself laughing out loud. #Genius

Shazza winks at me. 'I-I'm so sorry, I . . . yes, thanks, I'll let you know when I'm well enough to return. Bye.' She hangs up and gives me a high five. 'Sweet! I'm free!'

'That. Was. Amazing!' I laugh. 'How did you learn to make such authentic-sounding sick noises?'

'Practice. Every girl should know how to pull a sickie. It's one of life's vital skills!'

'And the thing with the tap? That was epic!'

'It's all about the details.' Shazza grins.

'So we've both successfully blagged the day off.' I grin back. 'Now what?'

'Now . . .' Shazza says dramatically, 'I want to see the future!'

10 SHAZZA

As Lucy and I walk through the town centre my eyes nearly pop out of their sockets. The future is majorly strange! I hardly recognize any of the stores — and what's with the gazillion coffee shops? Are people in the future, like, addicted to caffeine or something? And what's everyone *wearing*? Jeans are either so tight they look like leggings or so baggy they hang down, revealing people's pants!

'Gross! Are those guys trying to show off their underwear, or what?' I nudge Lucy.

'That's what Mum always says!' She laughs. 'It's fashion!'

'Really? Whatever happened to leg warmers and shoulder pads?'

'OMG! They disappeared, like, three decades ago — thank goodness!'

'Why do you keep calling me O.M.G.?' I ask as we cross the road in front of a bizarro car so tiny it looks more like a golf buggy. 'They're not even my initials.'

Lucy laughs. 'I'm not calling *you* OMG — it stands for Oh My . . . Goodness.'

'Oh right! So, like, *Oh My Giddy Aunt* would be OMGA?'

'Uh, I guess,' she says, leading me to a fancy-looking parade of shops.

'Sweet! So it's like, "OMGA, those shoes are so rad!" or, "OMGA, these clothes are so bogus!"' I stop dead as I catch sight of my reflection in a shop window.

'Kind of,' says Lucy. 'Though "rad" and "bogus" are pretty outdated.'

'So am I – look at me!' I groan, staring miserably at my frumpy beige dress, grandma shoes and boring handbag. And this was the best outfit I could find in Sharon's wardrobe. Majorly tragic! Grown-up Sharon definitely needs a kick up the fashion butt!

And a makeover.

11 LUCY

If listening to Shazza blag herself a sick day was in my top ten moments of all time, Shazza getting a makeover is *definitely* in my top five.

Especially as I'm getting one too! Finally I can go blonde! I have *always* wanted blonde hair. To be honest, anything's better than my long, lanky, mousy-brown locks. But would Mum ever let me dye them? #AsIf

Luckily today Shazza's in charge!

'Hi, I'm Lisa.' The spiky-haired hairdresser smiles at me as her colleague leads Shazza to the other end of the salon. 'What can I do for you today?'

'I'd like a blonde bob, please!' I beam. 'And can you pierce my ears too?'

'Well, you'll need parental consent for piercing and colouring,' Lisa says.

'No problem.' I grin. 'Mum!'

Shazza doesn't even look over.

'Mum!' I shout louder.

Still nothing. OMG, has she forgotten she's my mother?

'SHAZZA!'

'*What?*' She spins her chair around so quickly she nearly knocks her hairdresser over!

'Sorry! Just – you give permission for me to get my

38

hair dyed and ears pierced, don't you, *Mum*?'

'What? Oh yeah, whatever you want!' Shazza says excitedly. 'I didn't know they did ear-piercing here too!'

'Of course,' Lisa smiles. 'We do all kinds of body-piercing.'

'Rad! I'm gonna get my hair dyed too – what colour are you going?' Shazza asks. 'Wait! Don't tell me! It'll be a surprise! Let's have a big reveal when we're both done!'

'Ladies, we do recommend having an allergy test forty-eight hours before we dye your hair,' Shazza's hairdresser says. 'Just to be safe.'

My heart sinks. *Forty-eight hours?* Shazza will be gone by then!

'But . . . it's an emergency!' Shazza exclaims. 'We have a . . . um . . . wedding to go to. *Tonight!*'

'Oh.' The hairdresser looks startled. 'Well, we don't advise it, but if you sign a consent form—'

'Deal!' Shazza says quickly, winking at me.

I grin. I can't believe Mum was ever this cool!

12 SHAZZA

'Are you sure, Sharon?' my pretty blonde hairdresser says when I explain what I want. 'It's quite a change from your usual root-touch-up and trim . . .'

'That,' I say with a grin, 'is the whole idea . . . Michelle,' I add, reading her name badge.

'OK!' She stamps on a pedal and my chair actually *rises* – the future is so cool! My skin tingles with excitement. This is my first time in a proper salon! Ma usually cuts my hair at the kitchen table – I sit there with a tea towel round my neck, trembling with nerves as the kitchen scissors clack loudly and skim my skin, hardly daring to breathe in case she lops off an ear!

Today could not be more different. Michelle treats my hair with exotic-smelling dye, then brings me a pile of glossy women's magazines – *magazines*! Not comics! I cross my legs daintily like grown-ups do and pick up the top one – I feel totally sophisticated!

'Black coffee, no sugar, right?' Michelle asks.

'Ugh! No thanks!' I grimace. OK, so maybe I'm not *that* sophisticated! 'Um . . . have you got any Coke? Or squash? Or hot chocolate?'

'Sorry,' she says. 'Just tea, coffee or water.'

'Water would be great, thanks.' Seriously, what's with all the caffeine?

I flick through the magazine, but although it says it's a 'celebrity special', most of the featured 'celebrities' don't seem to have any profession at all — except being famous. How is that possible? HOW CAN YOU BE FAMOUS JUST FOR BEING FAMOUS?

Reading the captions underneath, loads of them are 'reality-TV stars' — what does that even mean? Is there some kind of *pretend* TV' these days? And why are nearly all of them ORANGE? Is it some kind of disease? Oompa-loompa-itis? Or some bizarro modern fashion?

OMGA . . . I hope Lucy hasn't decided to go orange!

13 LUCY

Butterflies flutter in my stomach as I stare at my reflection. I barely recognize myself! My new blonde bob curves neatly under my chin, and swings smoothly as I turn my head from side to side, admiring it from every angle. It's better than I ever dreamed! And the pretty heart studs glittering on my ears are the icing on the cake – and all without any blood or ice cubes! – though it did sting a bit.

'Happy?' Lisa smiles.

'Ecstatic!' I beam. 'I can't wait to show Sha— my mum.'

I hurry back to the waiting area, but she isn't there.

Suddenly an ear-splitting scream fills the air and I freeze. SHAZZA!?

I race towards the sound, my heart pounding. I should never have let her out of my sight. She's from the eighties! She's a twelve-year-old in a middle-aged person's body! She could be in danger!

'Where's my mum?' I cry, spotting Shazza's hairdresser at the counter. 'What's happening to her? Why aren't you with her?'

'She's out the back.' She points towards a door. 'But –'

I burst through the door before she can finish and find a large, heavily tattooed man leaning menacingly over a woman with bright red curly hair.

'Shazza?' I cry, uncertainly.

'Lucy!' Shazza wails, turning in her chair, her eyes streaming with tears.

'Get away from her!' I shout, grabbing the guy's bulky arm.

'Hey!' he yells, trying to shake me off.

'Shazza, run!' I scream.

'What?' She blinks at me. 'Why?'

'Because he . . . Because you . . .' I look from the man to Shazza. They both stare back at me blankly. 'Wait, what's going on? Why did you *scream*?'

'Sorry,' Shazza says, wiping her eyes. 'It was just a shock, that's all – I didn't expect it to hurt so much, but it's fine now.'

'What's fine? What hurt?'

She turns her head slightly and her nose glints in the light.

#OMG. It's pierced. Shazza got her nose pierced. Mum's gonna *kill* me!

'Isn't it rad?' Shazza squeals. 'I feel like a punk! And I love your earrings, Lucy – and your hair! You look totally grown-up!'

'Thanks!'

'D'you like mine?' She tosses her head and her tight red curls bounce wildly in every direction.

'I . . . it's . . . like, er, wow!' I force a smile. She looks like a cross between Sideshow Bob and a lion. 'Is that a *perm* . . . ?'

'No, it's just curled.' Shazza sighs as we head back to the counter. 'I really wanted a perm, but Michelle says they can't colour and perm at the same time.'

#Phew! I can just imagine Mum's face if she woke up with a perm! At least she can take a nose stud out or dye her hair again if she doesn't like it – but a perm is like, well . . . permanent!

'I can book you in for a perm in three weeks if you like, Sharon?' Michelle offers.

Shazza and I exchange glances.

'Um, I'm not sure I'll be here in three weeks,' Shazza says.

'Oh, going away, are you?'

'Kind of!' Shazza laughs and I smile.

'And are you paying for everything today, or shall I put it on your account?' Michelle asks.

'Oh – on my account would be awesome, thanks!' Shazza flashes me a thumbs-up.

'Would you like anything else?' Michelle smiles. 'Any shampoos or styling products, or—'

'Ooh! How about a heart nose stud to go with your earrings, Lucy?' Shazza interrupts, eyes gleaming.

'Er, no, thanks!' I say quickly.

'Are you sure? Or a lip ring? Or eyebrow stud? Rodney's really good – I know I screamed, but it only hurt for an instant, and—'

'I'm good!' I insist, backing away.

'We do tattoos too,' Michelle adds.

'*TATTOOS?!*' Shazza's eyes light up. 'Lucy, I've *always* wanted a tattoo!'

'*No way!*' I gasp, grabbing her arm and dragging her out of the salon.

Mum would *never* forgive me!

14 SHAZZA

We laugh all the way through our burger and chips.

'You should've seen your face when you stormed into the piercing room!' I giggle as I steal the last chip from Lucy's plate. 'I don't know who was more shocked – you or Rodney!'

'OMG, that is so not like me – usually I'm scared of my own shadow!' Lucy groans, burying her face in her hands. 'I don't know what came over me!'

'Aw, it was sweet. You were protecting your old mum!' I grin. 'And it was totally worth the pain. My nose-stud is so awesome – and OMGA, this is the best burger I've ever tasted!'

'It's the *first* burger I've ever seen you taste!' Lucy giggles, wiping ketchup off her chin. 'Mum's a vegetarian!'

'What?' I clap a hand over my mouth in horror – then burst out laughing. 'Whoops! Oh well! LTS!'

'*LTS?*' Lucy frowns.

'You know: life's too short!'

She laughs. 'You can't just make up your own acronyms, Shazza, that's not how it works! You mean "YOLO".'

'Huh?' Keeping up with future-speak is EXHAUSTING!

'You only live once!' Lucy grins. 'Or in your case, twice! So what d'you want to do next?'

'Ugh,' I groan. 'Next I need some new clothes. I cannot

spend another hour in Sharon's drab rags.'

'Preach!' Lucy cries.

'*What?*' Now I'm totally lost.

'It means, I totally agree!' She grins as the waiter brings our bill.

Lucy pulls a credit card out of Sharon's purse and my pulse quickens. Is she going to forge Sharon's signature? Is she expecting *me* to? I *am* Sharon after all – or will be – so it's not *technically* forgery . . . but I've, like, never even *seen* my future signature before – what if I get it majorly wrong? We could get in BIG trouble – we could even get arrested! Holy guacamole! My palms start to sweat, but to my surprise Lucy waves the card at a little black box that looks like a calculator and the waiter leaves.

'Ready to go?' Lucy pulls on her coat.

'Don't I have to . . . sign something?' I ask nervously.

'Nope!' She smiles. 'All done!'

'Phew!' I breathe, majorly relieved. After all, future-me would be pretty freaked out if she woke up in JAIL tomorrow!

15 LUCY

'Ooh, check out those funky tops!' Shazza cries, rushing over to a display of skin-tight Lycra in the window of the *Simply Teen* store. 'Aren't they rad?'

'Um, yeah, but . . .' I falter.

'But what?'

But the thought of my middle-aged mother wearing them is SO not. 'There's a much better place just down here.' I say quickly. 'I'll be your personal shopper!'

I hook my arm through Shazza's, hurry to the biggest department store in town and take her straight into the changing rooms. That way a) she can't choose any inappropriate clothes, and b) there's no risk of anyone I know seeing me shopping with my mother with her mad hair and nose-stud! #SocialSuicide

I hurry around the women's fashion section, and deliver several cool but age-appropriate outfits to Shazza – who has no idea how to wear any of them!

'This shirt's *way* too big!' she moans.

'It's a dress!' I laugh. 'Try it with a belt!'

'But now it looks like I forgot to put any trousers on!'

'It's *fashion*!' I protest.

'And these jeans don't have a zip!'

'They're jeggings!'

'What on earth are *jeggings*? And is this top

supposed to button up at the back?'

'Yes!' I sigh.

'Ugh! Aren't there any *normal* clothes out there?'

'Hang on, I'll grab some more.' I turn to go – then hear a familiar giggle.

I dive back inside Shazza's cubicle and yank the curtain closed – just in time! I peep through a gap, and see Megan, Nicole, Cara and Viv saunter into the changing rooms. I check my watch. School finished twenty minutes ago. I'd no idea it was so late.

'What's the matter?' Shazza frowns.

'Shh!' I hiss. 'It's the Megababes – the coolest girls in my year.'

'So?'

'So – I'm supposed to be ill! I'll get into heaps of trouble if they tell any teachers they've seen me shopping!'

Plus if they see me buying clothes with my mother they'll think I'm completely lame.

We both peer round the blue velvet curtain to see Megan twirling in front of the big mirror in the most beautiful sparkly white dress I've ever seen, her perfect blonde hair fanning out in a circle around her.

I sigh. 'I could never pull off a dress like that.'

'Of course you could!' Shazza scoffs. 'I'll get it for you.'

I block her way. 'You *cannot* go out there!'

'Why not? They don't know *I'm* supposed to be ill too, do they?' Shazza whispers.

'Well, no, but –'

With a swoosh of velvet she ducks past me out of the cubicle.

OMG. Who knows *what* she'll come back with?

16 SHAZZA

I wander round the store, past all the frumpy florals to a section filled with funky colours and trendy styles. That's *much* more like it. I find the white dress almost immediately – it's on display – then gleefully grab greedy armfuls of clothes before hurrying back to the changing rooms. The girls from Lucy's school have gone, so I kick her out of my cubicle while I get dressed.

'Can I look yet?' she asks impatiently.

'No! You've gotta wait for the big reveal!'

'And Mum calls *me* a drama queen!' she exclaims.

'Maybe it's genetic!' I laugh. 'OK . . . now! Ta-da!'

I sweep back the curtain and Lucy's jaw drops.

'OMG! What are you *wearing*?' she squeals.

'Aren't they gorgeous?' I grin, stepping out and twirling in front of the big mirror. I'm wearing a lime-green crop top, pink miniskirt and studded leather jacket. '*Much* better!'

'But . . . but you can't wear those!' Lucy gawps. 'They're for *teenagers*!'

'I *am* a teenager!' I protest. 'Well . . . almost.'

A woman checking her outfit in the mirror behind us looks at me strangely. Oops!

'Ha ha! Not for about twenty years, Mum!' Lucy laughs awkwardly, shoving me back into the cubicle and snapping the curtain shut. 'You have to get changed. Now.'

'But, *Lu-cy*, I don't *want* to wear frumpy *mum*-clothes!' I whine, slumping on to the stool.

'Shazza, you *are* a mum!' she retorts, hands on her hips. 'You're *my* mum!'

'Doesn't mean I have to act like it!' I stick my tongue out at her.

'You cannot go out in *public* like that!' Lucy wails. 'Please!'

'Why not?' I demand, folding my arms. 'Do I really look that bad?'

'Well . . . no, it's not that you look *bad*. It's just . . .' she hesitates, 'you won't fit in with other women your age.'

'Pah!' I scoff. 'Who wants to fit in anyway?'

'I do,' she whispers.

I frown. 'You don't want to be in that *Megababy* gang, do you?'

Lucy sighs. 'It's the Megababes. And, yes, *everyone* does. They're so pretty and popular.'

'You're pretty too!'

She rolls her eyes. 'Not *Megan*-pretty.'

'Rubbish!' I cry, hunting through my pile of clothes till I find the sparkly white dress. 'Come on, there's a spare cubicle now – put it on. I bet you'll look just as good in it as that Megan did – if not better!'

'I couldn't!' Lucy protests, hugging her arms. 'It's too short and too clingy and . . .'

'Try it,' I urge. 'I *dare* you.'

She raises an eyebrow. 'You *dare* me? How old are you?'

'Twelve.' I giggle. 'Come on, no one will see!'

Lucy hesitates, then smiles. 'OK. But only if you *promise* not to buy that skirt and crop top!'

'Fine!' I pout. 'But I'm keeping the jacket!'

'All right!' Lucy laughs. 'Deal!'

As she disappears into another cubicle, I hurriedly try on another outfit. Lucy's *bound* to love this hot-pink jeans, fluorescent-orange minidress and high-heeled boots combo!

She doesn't.

'My eyes!' She winces, peeking out from her cubicle, and my shoulders slump. 'The boots are cool though!' she adds quickly. 'Try that black lacy top with the pink jeans instead.'

'OK,' I say doubtfully. 'What about you? How's the dress?'

'Er . . . just give me a minute.'

But even when I've got changed again, Lucy's still not ready.

'Do you need help getting it on?' I call, wedging a

black fedora on top of my red curls.

'No,' she mutters. 'I'm going to take it off, it's no good—'

'*What?*' I yank back her curtain.

'Shazza!' Lucy shrieks shrinking into the corner. 'See – I can't wear this dress – it's far too short!' she moans, plucking at the hem, trying to pull it lower. 'And too tight!'

'Rubbish!' I cry. 'It fits you perfectly!'

'You really think so?' she says quietly.

'Lucy, look at yourself!' I drag her in front of the big mirror. 'You're totally gorgeous!'

The dress is beautiful. It's fitted at the waist, then flows gracefully down to just above Lucy's knees, shimmering like sunlight on water as she moves. Lucy smiles shyly at her reflection, then at me. 'Well *you* look gorgeouser.'

I beam. I love the outfit Lucy suggested – especially teamed with my new leather jacket and the funky fedora – I feel like Madonna!

She helps me put together a few more fab outfits. Then suddenly Sharon's handbag buzzes loudly!

'There's a bee in my bag!' I screech, backing away. 'And where's that weird music coming from?' I look around, confused as a pop song starts playing.

'It's your mobile,' Lucy says, hurrying into my cubicle carrying her dress.

'I have a *baby toy* in my bag?' I frown. 'OMGA!' My heart stops dead in utter horror. 'Do I . . . do I have a *baby*?'

'No!' Lucy laughs. 'It's a phone!' She pulls out a tiny metal object.

'But that's dinky! And it's *singing*!' I stare at it, gobsmacked.

Lucy looks at the screen. 'It's Dad.'

My eyes widen. 'I had no idea Danny was such a good singer!'

Lucy smiles. 'No, that's the ringtone, numpty. It's Dad *calling*.'

'Oh. OH!!' I stare at her, panic coursing through my veins. 'What should I say to him? Should I tell him what's happened?'

'No! I'll talk to him,' Lucy says quickly. 'Just give me a minute.' She drops the dress on my pile of clothes and hurries back into her own cubicle, pulling the curtain closed.

This is SO bizarro. I can't believe my future husband is talking to my future daughter on a singing phone the size of a credit card!

Ooh, that gives me an idea . . .

I check Lucy's still busy talking, then add her dress to my 'have-to-buy' collection, tiptoe carefully past her cubicle and hurry to the till — she's going to be so surprised!

'I'm keeping these on!' I tell the assistant, indicating my funky new outfit. There's no way I'm ever wearing Sharon's frumpy clothes again!

He sighs heavily – I don't know why, as *I'm* the one who has to be a major contortionist so he can scan all the labels! As he bags up my other clothes I pull out Sharon's shiny credit card. I love being a grown-up! I wave it like a magic wand over the little black calculator-box like Lucy did – this is so much fun!

'Insert your card, please,' the assistant says.

I blink. 'What?'

'Insert your card into the Chip-and-PIN machine, madam.'

I look around, but I can't see a pinball machine anywhere, and what have chips got to do with anything?

The assistant sighs AGAIN, then takes my card, slides it into the calculator-box and looks at me expectantly. OK . . . now what? Am I meant to add up my own bill?

'Now put your PIN in,' he says slowly and loudly.

I stare at him. Pin? What pin? A hairpin? My hands fly to my hair. I don't have one! What kind of bogus system is this? 'Can't I just sign something?' I ask anxiously.

He shakes his head, and a woman in the queue behind me huffs impatiently.

'Do you have a pin I can borrow?' I ask her desperately, and she looks at me like I'm crazy.

'Ms Dawes, this lady's forgotten her PIN!' the assistant calls loudly.

I panic. What's going to happen? What do I do? Where's Lucy?

Am I going to jail after all?

17 LUCY

Where's Shazza?

I swear I was only on the phone for five minutes tops, but there's no sign of her!

'Shazza!' I call, hurrying through the changing rooms. Has she gone into another cubicle? 'Shazza!'

I spot a flash of neon pink and yank back a curtain.

'Hey!' a half-dressed woman yelps.

'Sorry!' I try more cubicles until I've searched the whole of the changing rooms and am doing my best not to panic.

She can't have gone far. Right? *Right?*

I hurry back to the shop floor and scan the teen section. No sign of her.

I try the women's department. Still nothing.

Finally I run to the exit, hoping, wishing, praying she hasn't wandered off and got lost! OMG, what if she's lost her memory again? What if—

'*Lucy!*'

I spin around and spot an enormous queue by the till, headed by a red-faced Shazza. Thank goodness!

'There you are!' I cry, hurrying over. 'What were you *thinking*, wandering off? I was so worried!' I feel like we've swapped roles like in *Freaky Friday* after all!

'I'm sorry!' She flies into my arms. 'I-I wanted to

surprise you, but everything's just . . . just so confusing!'

'Why?' I ask, glancing at the flustered sales assistant and an older woman whose badge says 'Manager'. 'What's happened?'

'Madam, if you can't pay, you need to return the products,' the manager says tightly. 'Including the ones you're wearing!'

'Fine!' Shazza says miserably, unzipping her beloved leather jacket.

I stare at her. Is she going to strip off? In front of everyone?!

'Shazza, stop!' I cry. 'What's going on?!'

'I've searched through the whole handbag but I can't find any pins!' she wails.

'What?' I frown. *Pins?*

'There isn't even a cheque book!' she moans, plonking her fedora on the counter. 'And I don't have enough cash!'

Oh, I get it! Her PIN! 'Sorry, Shazza,' I whisper. 'I don't know your PIN number. We'll have to go and get some cash from the bank with your ID – after you've got changed *in the changing rooms.*' I grab her arm.

'Hang on.' She stares at me. 'It's a *number*?'

'Yes, madam, your four-digit *personal identification number.*' The assistant rolls his eyes.

'Why didn't you say so?!' Shazza cries, grabbing the machine.

'Yes, why *didn't* you?' The manager glares at the assistant, who cowers.

'What are you doing?' I ask as Shazza punches several buttons.

She frowns at the screen. '"Incorrect PIN"? But that's my favourite number! Unless . . .'

'You can't just *guess*!' I protest as she presses more numbers.

'Why not? Hmm, not my birthday either. I know!'

'Shazza, no! *You only get three tries!*' I lunge for the machine but I'm too late.

'"PIN accepted"!' Shazza crows triumphantly.

'What?' I stare at the machine as it prints the receipt. 'But how did you . . . what number was it?'

'It wasn't a number,' she whispers as she picks up her shopping bags. 'I mean, it *was*, but . . .'

'Huh?'

'The keys had letters on too.' Shazza smiles. 'It was your name.'

'My . . . wow.' A warm feeling tingles through me as I link my arm through hers. 'Come on, you, let's get out of here – and no more wandering off! I was worried sick! Anything could've happened to you!'

Shazza hangs her head. 'Sorry, Mum,' she says meekly – and we both burst out laughing.

'If only I'd had that musical-insect-phone thingy, I

could've called you,' Shazza says as I hand her mobile back to her.

'Right – except *I* haven't got one,' I sigh. 'Mum thinks I'm too young.'

'Wait, you don't have a phone?' Shazza gasps. 'But what if we get separated? How will I find you? Lucy, you totally, absolutely, definitely need a mobile phone! This instant!'

I grin.

It's raining as we head outside, but luckily uber-organized Mum *always* has an umbrella in her handbag. We huddle under it, arm in arm, as we hurry down the high street, giggling as I try to avoid the puddles – while Shazza splashes through them all!

'Ooh, look – someone's getting married!' she cries, stopping suddenly outside the registry office as a wedding party spills out in a flurry of umbrellas and confetti. 'I still can't believe I got married in a registry office. I still can't believe I'm *married*!'

'Come on.' I tug her arm. 'It's freezing.' *And let's get off the topic of marriage!*

'Hang on, they're all coming out – let's just wait for the bride. I want to see what modern wedding dresses look like!'

'You'll be waiting a long time,' I say with a smile.

'What do you mean?' She frowns.

I nod at the two guys getting showered with confetti as everyone else takes photos.

Shazza stares at me, gobsmacked. 'It's two *men* getting married? Is that legal?'

'Course.' I smile. 'Same-sex marriage is no big deal these days. I mean, some people still have issues, but why shouldn't everyone be allowed to marry the person they love?'

'Well, of course, they should – they totally should. That's . . . wow, that's awesome.' She beams. 'It's a whole new world!'

'No, it's just not the eighties any more, Shazza!' I laugh.

Shazza's mind continues to be blown in the phone shop. 'Why are all the mobiles named after *fruit*?' she asks. 'They're not even fruit-shaped!'

'That's what Mum always says,' I giggle. Maybe she hasn't changed that much after all.

'They're so small – and so cheap!' Shazza continues.

This time I laugh out loud. 'That is so NOT what Mum says!'

'In the eighties they're like, thousands of pounds! And majorly huge – like bricks!'

'Really?' I smile. 'So . . . ninety quid's a bargain then, huh?'

'Totally!'

OMG, I love Shazza!

Unfortunately, now that it's stopped raining Shazza sticks out like a sore thumb as we walk through town. Loads of people turn and stare, and I can't really blame them – especially as she keeps running around and pointing at things, shouting weird eighties words! #Embarrassing

I pull my hood up, my cheeks burning, hoping we don't bump into anyone we know – I would never live this down.

And neither would Mum, I realize suddenly. It's not just my reputation at stake.

I grab Shazza's arm. 'I'm tired – let's go home.'

'What? No way!' she protests, pulling free. 'I'm only here for a day – I want to make the most of it!'

My heart sinks.

'Come on, if you'd just travelled here from the eighties, what would you do?'

I think fast. 'How about a movie?'

'Awesome!'

'Cool!' I grin. No one will be able to see us in the dark!

'No *way* is this a cinema!' Shazza gasps as we walk into the multiplex. 'It's enormous!'

'It has to be, to fit twelve screens,' I explain.

'OMGA! *Twelve screens?* No way!' Shazza squeals, running towards the ticket counter like an overhyped toddler.

'Way!' I grin, racing after her. 'So what do you wanna see?'

'Lucy?' calls a familiar voice. 'Is that you?'

I turn to see the Megababes. Oh crumpets! So much for keeping out of sight . . .

'Nice hair!' Megan says as they join the queue behind us. 'I *almost* didn't recognize you!'

'Oh. Thanks!' I smile. Wait, that *was* a compliment, wasn't it?

'You must be Lucy's mum! I love your nose-stud, Mrs Andrews!' Megan beams at Shazza.

'Thanks!' she replies. 'Call me Shazza.'

'*Shazza?*' Megan's eyes widen. 'Wow! Lovely to meet you, *Shazza*. How *sweet*! I don't think my mum's taken me to the cinema since I was about . . . eight?'

The other Megababes snigger, and Nicole whispers, 'Lame.'

#KillMeNow

'So you must be Megan,' Shazza says sweetly.

'I am!' Megan flicks her silky blonde hair smugly.

'Well, I'm so sorry your mum doesn't have time for you, Megan,' Shazza says, 'but at least you have your clones.'

Megan's smile slips. 'My *what?*'

'Your lovely clothes!' Shazza smiles. 'They're gorgeous!'

'Oh.' Megan blinks, looking confused. 'Thanks.'

I bite down hard on my lip to hide my smile.

'So, what movie are you girls seeing today?' Shazza asks.

'The new romcom,' Nicole replies, nodding at a poster behind the counter of a loved-up teenage couple.

'How *sweet*!' Shazza grins.

'Next!' the ticket guy calls to us.

'Two for *Mutant Zombie Vampires*, please,' Shazza says. The Megababes gasp and I stare at Shazza. *Mutant Zombie Vampires* is a fifteen!

'Um, do you have any ID?' the ticket guy asks.

Shazza raises an eyebrow. 'Young man, how *old* do I look to you?'

It takes all my willpower not to burst out laughing.

'Uh, I meant your, er, daughter,' he says, his ears flushing bright red. 'Is she fifteen?'

'Do you really think I'd bring her if she wasn't?' Shazza narrows her eyes.

'Um, n-no, of course not!' he stutters. 'But I-I'm really meant to see ID . . .'

'I am her mother. I think I know how old my own daughter is.'

'Of course, it's just –' He looks around desperately for

65

help, but all the other staff are busy serving customers. 'We're meant to check—'

'Are you calling me a *liar*?' Shazza demands, her voice dangerously quiet.

'No! No, of *course* not!'

'Well, then! Two tickets, please – at the front!'

Utterly defeated, the poor guy meekly obeys.

'That –' I giggle as we walk away – 'was totally awesome!'

And the most awesome thing of all is the look on the Megababes' faces as we walk away. *Now* who's lame?

'Wait!' the ticket guy calls after us. 'Don't forget your glasses!'

'Glasses?' Shazza spins round. 'You cheeky—'

'Thank you!' I say, hurriedly collecting the 3D glasses he's holding before Shazza can ruin everything.

'Oh . . . I thought he was calling me old,' she whispers as I steer her away from the Megababes. 'Why do we need these? Are they a free gift?'

'No,' I hiss. 'You wear them to watch the movie.'

'*Really?* Why? Are future cinema screens, like, really tiny? Or are we miles from the screen? And these look more like sunglasses – why on earth do we need sunglasses *inside*? In the *dark*? This makes absolutely no sense!'

'Wait and see.' I grin. This is going to be classic.

18 SHAZZA

'AAAARGH!' I scream as the zombie literally crawls OUT OF THE SCREEN!

'Shush!' Lucy hisses.

'But he's coming to get me!' I whimper. The zombie's slimy rotting hand reaches straight for my throat and I grab a shopping bag to shield myself. Is this what happens in future cinemas? The characters actually ATTACK you? 'We have to get out of here!'

'Shhhh, it's OK!' Lucy whispers. 'It's just the glasses!'

The glasses? I take them off and the zombie instantly becomes blurry, the screen flat again.

'B-but how? And *why*? Are they *magic*?' I gaze at them in awe.

'Be quiet!' someone behind us scolds.

Suddenly Lucy squeals.

'What happened?' I squint at the screen, but it's hard to make out what's going on without the weird glasses.

'The girl's gone into the haunted house!' Lucy whispers nervously.

'What a doofus!' I hiss. 'Now what's happening?'

'Please BE QUIET!' the man behind us chides. I turn and stick my tongue out at him and his jaw drops in surprise. Oh yeah, I'm meant to be, like, forty-something. Oops.

When I turn back I've no idea what's happening, so

finally, hesitantly, I put the glasses back on again . . .
BIG MISTAKE!

'AAAAARGH!' I shriek as a chainsaw-wielding vampire lunges towards me, laughing manically. That's it – I can't take any more! I grab my bags, jump out of my seat and flee, Lucy hot on my heels.

'I'm going to have nightmares for weeks!' I cry, bursting out of the cinema on to the dark street outside. 'Why would anyone want to watch *that*?' I shudder. 'It's *horrible*!'

Lucy laughs, pulls my weird glasses off my face, tosses them in a bin, and hooks her arm through mine. 'Let's go home.'

19 LUCY

On the way back we pick up essentials (sweets, crisps, doughnuts) from the supermarket – or, as Shazza called it, the 'super-duper-market'! ('Holy guacamole! Since when did shops become the size of *airports*? How much food do people *need*? And is that a television? And clothes? OMGA, do they sell EVERYTHING?')

Shopping has never been so much fun!

Back home I tuck into the sweets while Shazza parades around her bedroom in her new outfits, like a model on a catwalk.

'Mum is so going to flip when she sees all her new clothes!' I giggle as Shazza strikes a pose.

'You think she – I – won't remember buying them?' Shazza frowns.

I shrug. 'I don't know what she – you – will remember. I hope you don't forget everything though.'

'I'm sure I'll love them,' Shazza says, pouting at herself in the mirror. 'After all, I'm still me, right?'

'Right . . .'

But really the only resemblance between Shazza and my mother is purely physical, and since her makeover even that's faded a lot. If her voice didn't sound just the same and if she didn't have the same eyes and wrinkles, I wouldn't believe she was actually the same person at all.

My phone bleeps from where it's charging on the bedside table. It's Kimmy, accepting my TeenSpace friend request. I can't believe I can finally go on social media!

How RU? Hope UR feeling Bettr

I feel a twinge of guilt that she thinks I'm ill – we don't usually keep any secrets from each other – but it's late now and it'd take ages to explain about skipping school and my magic wish and Mum turning into Shazza, and to be honest, I just want to make the most of the time I've got left with Shazza; after all, she'll be gone tomorrow. I'll tell Kimmy all about it then!

Suddenly Zak's picture pops up on my phone as he updates his profile. He looks even more gorgeous than ever – if that's possible. If only *he'd* accept my friend request . . . but of course he probably has absolutely no idea who I am.

'Ooh, who's that?' Shazza says, peering over my shoulder.

'That's Zak.' I smile. 'The fittest guy at school.'

'He does a lot of sport?'

'No, *fit* – you know, good-looking.'

'Oh right!' She flops down next to me on the bed. 'So is he your *boyfriend*?' She winks.

'I wish!' I laugh. 'Besides, Mum thinks he's too old for me. He's just turned fourteen.'

'Pah!' Shazza laughs. 'Trev's, like, fourteen and a *half*.'

#JawDrop. So not only did Mum have a boyfriend when she was my age, he was more than two years older than her! Hypocrite!

'So . . . have you asked Zak out?' Shazza asks.

'As if!' I laugh. 'I've never even spoken to him!'

'What? Why *not*?'

'Because . . . whenever he's nearby my throat just completely dries up and my legs turn to jelly!'

'Must be love!' Shazza swoons.

'It's hopeless!' I sigh, gazing at his picture again. 'He has no idea I even exist!'

'Then make him notice you!' Shazza sits up. 'You just need a bit more confidence, Lucy – you have to take your destiny into your own hands! Worked for me. I got fed up of waiting for Trev to ask me out, so finally I just went up and asked *him* out.'

'You did not!' I can't believe Mum was ever this feisty.

'Did so!' She grins.

'I could never do that!' I gasp. 'Just the thought of it makes me dizzy!'

'Well, you have to do *something* to get Zak's attention!'

'Actually –' I hesitate – 'there is this Black and White Ball . . .'

Shazza's eyes light up. 'Awesome! And I know *exactly* what you should wear!' She grabs one of the shopping

71

bags and pulls out the sparkly white dress I tried on earlier. I can't believe it!

'OMG! Shazza, no way!'

'Way!' She beams.

'Thank you *so* much!' I squeal. 'It's *perfect* for the ball!' Then my heart sinks. 'But Mum'll never let me keep it. She'll return it to the shop tomorrow.'

'In that case . . . whoops!' Shazza rips the label off and tears it into tiny pieces. 'She can't return it now!'

I gasp. '*Shazza!* It was so expensive!'

'So what? Lucy, you're my daughter and this ball is majorly important. I mean, Zak could be, like, *The One*! If this dress gets him to notice you, it could change your whole entire life!'

I can't believe it. My mother finally understands me. Tears filling my eyes, I throw my arms around her. 'Thank you!'

'You're welcome!' She laughs. 'And thank *you* for wishing me here, Luce. I'm so psyched I got to meet you!'

'Me too.' I beam. 'Today's been uber-amazing.'

But tomorrow Mum will be back. She'll return my phone. She'll say I can't go to the ball, and she DEFINITELY won't let me date Zak.

And worst of all, Shazza will be gone.

20 SHAZZA

I can't sleep. My nose-stud might look cool but it's really irritating me, so I take it out – but every time I close my eyes I see horrible zombies! And strange shadows keep flitting over the ceiling. And it's so *noisy*. Cars are still driving past, even though it's really late! And I can't get comfy – this bed feels weird and this nightdress smells funny, but the main problem is . . . I don't have Zebby. I haven't slept a single night without my toy zebra in my entire life. Or my night light . . .

I climb out of bed and tiptoe into the hallway. I'm sure Lucy won't mind if I put the light on . . . just so I don't, like, trip over anything if I need the loo. I fumble for the light switch and suddenly something touches my arm!

I scream, jump backwards, fall over and squeal even louder as I curl up into a defenceless ball. *It's a ZOMBIE! They've come for me!*

Suddenly the light clicks on.

'Mum? Are you OK?'

I peer up nervously. 'Lucy?' Of course it's Lucy! Duh! 'Um, yeah. It's just it's, like, majorly dark and I couldn't get to sleep . . .'

Lucy's face lights up. 'You're still Shazza?'

'Yes.' I smile. 'Actually, um, as we're both still awake,

and I'm only here for tonight, maybe we could have, like, a sleepover?'

She smiles. 'Are you scared of the zombies?'

'*Yes!*' I confess. 'This house is majorly strange and super-scary and what if the zombies are, like, *under my bed*?'

Lucy laughs. 'Well then, you'd better come in.' She flings her door wide open.

'Thank you!' I dive on to her bed – and land on something lumpy. I can't believe my eyes. '*Zebby?*'

He's much tattier, but he still feels – and smells – the same. Finally there's something familiar in this weird world.

'You gave him to me when I was a baby.' Lucy smiles, leaning over to stroke his soft, worn ears. 'He was my favourite toy. I've grown out of the others, but Zebby's just, well . . .'

'Special.' I beam, handing him to Lucy as she climbs into bed beside me.

She shakes her head. 'You keep him tonight. He'll help protect you from the zombies. He's a very fierce little zebra.'

I smile. 'He is.' I snuggle down, take a deep breath of Zebby's lavender scent and feel instantly at home.

TUESDAY

21 LUCY

As sunlight fills my room I yawn and stretch – then nearly jump out of my skin as someone suddenly snores loudly beside me! I completely forgot about Shazza! She's fast asleep, her new red curls splayed over my pillow, Zebby tucked under her arm.

I smile, remembering how we lay here for hours last night, talking about anything and everything. I told her all about Zak and Kimmy and school – things I've never told Mum, things Mum just wouldn't understand. But Shazza did. It was almost like having a sister. From the eighties . . .

#Crazy

Suddenly she yawns and my heart beats faster. Will she remember? Or will it be like yesterday never happened? I hold my breath.

'Lucy?' She blinks sleepily. Then her eyes fly open. 'Holy guacamole, I'm still here!'

I gasp. '*Shazza?*'

'I'm still in the future!' she cries, gazing around the room. 'Isn't this rad?' She throws her arms around me and I hug her back tightly. This is amazing!

But suddenly my joy is tinged with fear.

Why hasn't she changed back to Mum? *When* will she change back?

What if she *never* changes back?

22 SHAZZA

'I don't get it. Why are you calling the doctor? I feel fine!' I protest as Lucy picks up her mobile.

'Shazza, you're a twelve-year-old in a middle-aged body! That's not exactly normal!' Lucy reasons.

'Well, no – it's magic!' I exclaim.

'But what if it's *not*?' Lucy bites her lip. 'I only wished you here for a day, after all . . .'

'Well, sorry for outstaying my welcome!' I huff, folding my arms.

'I didn't mean it like that!'

'I thought you *liked* having me here?'

'Shazza!' Lucy grabs me in a hug. 'I LOVE having you here. Yesterday was one of the best days of my life!'

'Really?' I say, pulling back and scanning her earnest face.

'Really,' she insists. 'I just want to make sure you're OK. OK?'

I roll my eyes. 'Fine!'

But apparently luck's not on her side.

'There's no appointments until Thursday,' Lucy sighs, hanging up.

'Awesome!' I jump up. There's so much of the future still to explore! 'So what shall we do today?'

'Well . . .' Lucy pulls a face. 'I *have* to go to school.

The Megababes saw me at the cinema yesterday so they know I'm not ill.'

'Bogus,' I groan, my excitement popping like a balloon as I flop back down on the bed. 'So, like, what am *I* supposed to do all day?'

Lucy shrugs. 'Watch TV? Go online?'

'Go where?' I frown.

'On the Internet,' Lucy explains.

I blink. 'What's the Internet?'

23 LUCY

'Oh my giddy, giddy aunt, my mind is literally BLOWN!' Shazza cries, her eyes like saucers as I open up different websites on Mum's laptop in the lounge.

'So you can watch TV, films or find any information you like,' I explain. 'Just type what you want here, then press Search.'

'By clicking the . . . oh, don't tell me.' She squeezes her eyes shut. 'It's some kind of rodent . . . the rat?'

'The mouse.' I smile.

She giggles. 'You future dudes have such bizarro names for things.'

I laugh, then notice the time on the computer's clock. 'Crumpets, I've got to go.' I jump off the sofa and pull on my big furry trapper hat and coat. 'See you after school, OK? Remember, don't go outside, open the door or answer the phone – unless it's me.'

Shazza rolls her eyes. 'Just like Snow White.'

'Exactly!' I wink. 'If you need me for anything, just call my mobile like I showed you. It'll be on silent – we're not meant to have mobiles at school – so leave a message and I'll ring back as soon as I can, OK?'

'All right already! Don't have a cow, dude!' Shazza says, in a terrible attempt at an American accent.

I raise an eyebrow. 'A *cow*?'

Shazza laughs. 'I'll be fine!'

I hope so. I grab my school bag and hurry outside, pulling up my hood against the October drizzle. I check my mobile to make sure it's on, then I hesitate. Is it really safe to leave Shazza home alone? A twelve-year-old girl from 1985, loose in the twenty-first century? Who knows what trouble she could get into? *Wait, who's the parent here anyway?*

#RoleReversal

'Lucy!'

I turn to see Kimmy running towards me.

'I'm so glad you're feeling better!' she cries, hugging me tight. 'I rang your house after school to check on you, but there was no answer.'

'Sorry, I—'

'Of course, I could've called you on your cool new smartphone if I'd known!' she squeals, spotting my mobile. 'Wow!'

'Mum bought it for me,' I explain, as we walk towards school.

'*Really?*' Kimmy raises an eyebrow. 'I thought she was uber-against you having a mobile?'

'Well . . . she's changed!' I grin. 'You're never gonna believe what happened—'

'What happened?' Megan cuts in as the Megababes walk up beside us. 'Ooh, nice phone!'

She snatches it from my hand.

'Hey, give that back!' Kimmy demands.

'Chill, Chung, I'm just looking. Lucy doesn't mind, do you?' Megan says sweetly.

'I . . . um . . . no?' I say helplessly.

'See?' Megan smiles smugly as Kimmy frowns. 'It was lovely to meet your mum last night, Lucy. How was *Mutant Zombie Vampires*?'

'What?' Kimmy stares at me. 'I thought you were ill yesterday?'

'Oops, did I put my foot in it?' Megan's eyes gleam. 'You certainly didn't look very ill, Lucy, especially with your chic new hairstyle.'

'What new hairstyle?' Kimmy's frown deepens.

'You haven't *seen*?' Megan nods at Nicole, who pulls my hood down and my hat off.

Kimmy gasps. 'What did you *do*?'

My hands fly to my hair. 'Don't you like it?'

'Well, yes, but I liked it before!' Kimmy says. Suddenly her jaw drops. 'OMG, are those *earrings*?'

'Gorgeous, huh? What a makeover!' Megan gushes. 'Selfie time! All the blondes together!' She pulls me into a group shot with the Megababes and I beam at the camera – trying to ignore Kimmy scowling at us.

Megan checks the result, smiles and shows it round. I can hardly believe it. *Me* in a photo with the *Megababes*!

'Nice camera,' she says. 'But you could really do with some decent tunes. The Star-Gazers album? *Really?*' She taps the phone and my favourite band begins to play.

Nicole smirks. 'Lame.'

My cheeks burn. 'That was already on there,' I lie. I downloaded it last night.

'Ugh, don't you hate when they do that?' Megan grimaces. 'You don't mind if I borrow your phone till the end of the day, do you, Luce? Surfing YouTube might *just* keep me sane through double maths!'

'Er, actually—'

'I'd be MEGA grateful,' Megan interrupts, batting her eyelashes. 'Plus I could download some decent music for you.'

Kimmy narrows her eyes. 'Like she needs your help.'

Megan scowls at her.

'I'm sorry,' I say, 'but I really need my phone today.'

'What a shame!' Megan pouts. 'Cos you know mobile phones aren't *allowed* in school, are they?' She tosses it to Nicole.

'Nope,' Nicole says, throwing it to Cara. 'Why's that, Cara?'

'It's probably because it could get lost,' Cara says, chucking it to Viv.

'Or broken,' adds Viv, throwing it back to Megan.

'Or nicked.' Megan grins.

'Give it back!' Kimmy growls, lunging at Megan and accidentally knocking the phone out of her hand.

'No!' I cry as it plummets towards a puddle . . . but suddenly, from out of nowhere, a hand catches it.

I look up and my heart stops dead. It's Zak!

'Is this yours?' he asks, his chocolate eyes locking on mine, leaving me unable to think or speak. Or breathe.

I nod dumbly.

'Great reflexes, Zak!' Megan coos. 'Must be all that football training, huh?' She flicks her hair, but Zak's frowning at my phone. He turns the volume up and I suddenly realize my favourite album is still playing!

#KillMeNow

Zak tilts his head to one side. 'Is this the Star-Gazers?'

I nod helplessly, my cheeks blazing as my heart crashes through the floor. Great. My rubbish taste in music has ruined my chances before I've even managed to utter a single word. So much for taking control of my destiny!

He raises a perfect eyebrow. 'Good taste.'

#JawDrop

As he passes me my phone, his hand brushes mine and a tingle shoots straight up my spine, making me dizzy.

'See you around.' He winks and my legs turn to mush.

OMG! This is the best day of my life! Zak looked at me! Zak spoke to me!

This is *insane*!

24 SHAZZA

This is INSANE. I munch through a packet of crisps as I stare at the computer screen, majorly flabbergasted. How has the world changed *so much* in just a few decades? I can't believe you can find out anything about everything with just a click of a button. This would've made my homework WAY easier! And then there's online shopping, and movies, and games – it's endless!

I look up my favourite pop stars and am horrified to see that most of them are really old and wrinkly – or dead! OMGA, Michael Jackson's *dead*? I click a picture, and a video of his greatest hits starts playing – half of which I've never ever *heard* before! They're songs from the future! This is SO RAD!

I crank the volume up and dance around the living room, but soon I'm totally puffed out. *What's wrong with me?* Then I catch sight of myself in the mirror. Ugh! *That's* what's wrong – I'm not a twelve-year-old, rocking out. I'm a red-faced middle-aged woman! I slump into a chair, tossing the packet of crisps in the bin.

What happened to me? Why didn't I go back to the eighties this morning? How will I get home? What if I'm trapped here forever? SO MANY QUESTIONS!

Suddenly it hits me – the Internet! It's *bound* to know the answer! It knows everything!

I pull the computer on to my lap and type in 'Waking up in the future'. A long list of sci-fi films and books pops up, then – holy guacamole! – an article about a woman just like me!

I read it quickly, learning that she had a form of amnesia that usually passes in time, but can recur, and it's caused by . . . *emotional stress*.

My mind races. *Amnesia?* That means . . . it wasn't magic after all. I've just lost my memory . . . *of the last thirty-odd years!* This is so bizarro! On one hand, I'm kind of gutted that I haven't travelled through time, but on the other, I'm majorly relieved to discover that there might be a way to fix this – I don't fancy being a twelve-year-old stuck in a middle-aged body forever!

All I need to do is work out what Sharon was stressed about and fix it . . . but besides being old, unfit and severely lacking in fashion sense, she seems to have a pretty good life: a nice house, a cool-if-underconfident daughter, good job, lovely husband . . . What could she *possibly* be stressed about? I tap the mouse absent-mindedly as I rack my brains – and suddenly all the websites disappear. Oh fudgeballs, what have I done?

The screen is now dotted with little pictures with writing underneath. I scan them quickly, then spot one that reads 'Emergencies'. This is totally an emergency! I click on it and a whole new screen pops up, filled with little white rectangles labelled: 'Home Insurance'; 'Car Insurance'; 'Travel Insurance'; 'Lucy's School Round Robin' . . .

I remember these – we've got one for my class too. If there's ever, like, an emergency, each parent rings the next one on the list, who does the same until everyone's got the message.

I click the square and a list of names and numbers appears. There's Lucy's friend Kimmy's number, and Megan's . . .

I think of Lucy's longing expression when she saw Megan and her clones hanging out yesterday, of how she's too shy to even talk to Zak, and how sad she sounded as we lay in bed last night when she told me about Kimmy never having time for her any more . . . If anything, it's *Lucy* who's unhappy.

Maybe that's it. *That's* why Sharon's stressed out? She's worried about *Lucy*? Of course!

And I know *exactly* how to fix everything.

25 LUCY

'I'm glad you're feeling better today, Lucy,' my English teacher says as I walk past her in the corridor. 'And I like your hair!'

'Thanks, Ms Banks – you too!' Her long black trademark braids are twisted into a funky sideways knot, and she looks amazing. She might be a teacher, but she's pretty cool – and today, it seems, so am I! All day, girls I don't even know have been coming up to compliment me on my new look. Everyone seems to love it!

Except Kimmy.

By the time I'd finished talking to Zak she'd disappeared, and she's been giving me the cold shoulder all day, which is uber-frustrating as I'm *bursting* to tell her about Shazza! But she's deliberately sat at a different table to me in every lesson, disappeared at break and played sports all through lunch (surprise, surprise).

I finally catch up with her heading back to the sports block after school. 'Kimmy, wait!' I call, running up to her. 'Can you come over to my house?'

'I've got netball practice,' she replies, walking away.

'Can't you miss it just this once?' I plead, following her.

She shakes her head. 'We've got a match tomorrow.'

'But I need to talk to you about yesterday!' I beg. 'Please, let me explain!'

Kimmy glances at her watch, then sighs. 'You've got five minutes.'

'OK! Well, on Sunday night Mum and I had this mahoosive argument about whether or not I could go to the ball and I made a wish—'

'A *wish*?' Kimmy interrupts. 'Like Cinderella? Lucy, you know there's no such thing as magic, right?'

'Well, that's what I thought as well!' I exclaim. 'But on Monday morning when I woke up Mum had *changed*!'

'You mean changed her mind?' she scoffs. 'That's not *magic*!'

'No, that's not what I—'

'OMG! *What* is *that*?' Kimmy cries, staring at something behind me.

I follow her gaze to a bright pink limousine parked just outside the school gates. *It's so cool!*

'That's so tacky.' Kimmy winces. 'I bet it's here for the Megabimbos, It's their garish signature colour after all.'

Sure enough, the back door opens and Megan leaps out – but to my surprise she runs straight towards us, grabbing me in a tight hug that nearly knocks me off my feet.

'I'm outta here!' Kimmy rolls her eyes.

'No! Wait!' I call after her.

'I'm late, Luce!' Kimmy yells over her shoulder as she hurries away. 'See ya.'

'Lucy Andrews –' Megan pulls back from me, her eyes sparkling – 'your mum is MEGA-cool!'

'Uh . . . *really*?' A trickle of fear runs down my spine. Shazza was supposed to stay inside, keep a low profile . . .

'I can't believe she organized a retro pizza party for all the girls in our class – and a limo to pick us up!'

'She did *what*?' I gasp. OMG. That is the *polar opposite* of keeping a low profile!

Megan's hand flies to her mouth. 'Was it supposed to be a surprise? I didn't know anything about it till just now, but she's cleared it with all our parentals, and I've been rounding everyone up since I know, well, *everyone*.' She beams as she flicks her hair. 'And you're the last one! So let's go!'

'Wait – what about Kimmy?' I turn towards the sports block. 'I should tell her.'

'She looked pretty busy to me,' Megan says. 'Why don't you text her and she can come over later?'

'I dunno . . .'

'Hey,' Megan interrupts. 'Is that Zak talking to your mum?'

'*What?*' I spin round quickly.

#Disaster!

26 SHAZZA

Lucy's face is priceless – she's so surprised! This is the best plan ever! I wave across the playground at her, when suddenly I notice a teenage boy standing beside me.

'Hi,' he says.

'Hi.' I smile, curling a strand of hair around my finger. Boys in the future might have bizarro hair and baggy trousers, but they're still *really* cute.

'You're Lucy's mum, right?' he says.

'Oh. Um. Yeah.' I clear my throat, reminding myself I'm old enough to be *his* mother too. Plus he looks kind of familiar . . . 'OMGA! You must be Zak!'

His brown eyes flicker. 'How did you know that?'

'Oh, er, Lucy tells me about everyone at school.' I shrug in what I hope is a nonchalant way. I've read about being nonchalant around boys. I'm still not *quite* sure what it means though . . .

He nods. 'Cool jacket, Mrs A.'

'Oh, Lucy's the cool one,' I insist, seizing my chance to big her up. 'She chose it.'

'She's got good taste.' Zak smiles.

In boys too, I think. 'Lucy's totally awesome,' I gush. 'She's so smart, and funny, and kind. We're more like friends than mother and daughter!'

'Sha— *Mum!*' Lucy runs over. 'What's up?'

'Nothing!' I insist. 'I was just talking to Zak.'

'Hey, Luce.' Zak nudges her gently on the arm and Lucy's cheeks flush bright pink – it is SO cute!

A car horn beeps.

'Gotta go!' Zak grins. 'It was nice to meet you, Mrs A. See ya, Luce!'

As soon as he's out of earshot I turn to Lucy. 'OMGA! He is so phat.'

'What?' Lucy glares at me. 'Zak's not fat!'

'No – "*phat*" – you know. Like cool!'

Lucy shakes her head. 'What happened to keeping a low profile?' she hisses. 'And what's with the limo? And the party?'

'Don't you like it?' I ask anxiously. What if I've got this majorly wrong? What if she hates it?

But Lucy's faces breaks into a grin. 'I love it!'

'Hooray!' I beam, flinging open the door. 'Tonight, Cinderella, I am your fairy godmother!'

27 LUCY

'This is MEGA-fun!' Megan cries, copying Shazza as she teaches everyone to moonwalk around the lounge. I feel as if I've stepped into a time warp. Shazza's wild clothes and hair fit in perfectly now she's given everyone eighties makeovers – complete with side ponytails and bright make-up – while Michael Jackson struts around on YouTube on the TV.

How does she do it? If I tried to throw a party, no one would come, and anyone who did would think it was uber-lame – especially if I chose an eighties theme! But everyone loves Shazza, and Megan seems to be her new best friend – and mine too.

'Come on, Lucy!' Megan calls. 'It's better than Just Dance!'

'What's Just Dance?' Shazza asks.

'You know, the Wii game?'

'The *wee game*?' Shazza looks horrified, and I laugh. As I join in with everyone moving in sync, I finally feel like I belong. If only Kimmy was here, everything would be perfect.

Suddenly the doorbell rings.

'Pizza!' Shazza cries, and everyone cheers as I hurry to get the door.

But it's Kimmy!

'You came!' I beam.

'Yeah,' she mutters. 'I got your text . . .'

'Woo! Madonna!' Megan cries as 'Material Girl' starts playing and everyone instantly starts doing the dance moves Shazza taught us earlier.

'*What* is happening?' Kimmy looks around uncertainly. Her eyes widen as she spots Shazza.

'Come on, Kimmy!' I smile. 'The moves are really easy – or I'd never have got the hang of them! You just put your arms like this, then—'

'I'm OK,' she interrupts, backing away from me. 'This is more of a *blonde* song anyway. Can I have a drink?'

'Course,' I say, frowning as I follow her into the kitchen. 'What's the matter?'

She rounds on me. 'What's the *matter*? You throw a party without me, and then *you* ask *me* what's the matter?'

'I didn't know about the party!' I protest. 'Mum organized it!'

Kimmy raises an eyebrow. 'Since when does your mum organize surprise parties?'

'That's what I've been trying to tell you – she's changed!' I say, pouring cherryade into plastic cups.

'No kidding – she's really got into the eighties theme, huh?' Kimmy says, eyeing suspiciously the neon-pink drink I've handed her.

'You have no idea!' I shake my head. 'Kimmy, she says she's *from* the eighties!'

'Well . . . she *is*!' Kimmy shrugs.

'No, that's not what I mean—'

'So that's what's going on?' she interrupts. 'Your mum decided to get a makeover so you got one too?'

'It's more than just a makeover!' I protest.

'That's what I'm worried about!'

'Me too!' I cry. 'I mean, it was great at first, but now I'm getting worried because it's lasted longer than a day, and what if—'

'What has?' Kimmy frowns. 'Your hair dye? Was it meant to wash out?'

'What? No!' *Why doesn't she ever listen?* 'Mum's weird behaviour! I'm really worried about her!'

Kimmy rolls her eyes. 'Don't be. Dad says everyone goes a bit wild after a divorce. It's normal.'

Normal?! I stare at her, confused. Hasn't she heard a word I've said?

'But that doesn't explain *your* weird behaviour,' she adds.

'Huh?' I blink in surprise. '*My* weird behaviour?'

'Yes! Your bimbo makeover's one thing, but—'

'My *what*?' I gasp, my whole body bristling. 'Just because I've dyed my hair doesn't make me a *bimbo*! Is that what you meant when you called that Madonna song "blonde"?'

'Material Girl?' Kimmy scoffs, dumping her untouched drink in the sink. 'Life's about more than clothes and shopping, Lucy. Or at least it should be.'

'Kimmy, it's just a song!' I scowl at her. 'It's classic Madonna! We used to dance to "Holiday" all the time!'

'Yeah, goofing around, changing the words and taking the mickey!'

I fold my arms tightly, trying to contain my anger. 'Well, I *like* Madonna.'

She raises an eyebrow. 'Really?'

'Yes! Really!' I snap. '*And* I LOVED the pink limo.'

'Wow. Maybe you should join the Megabimbos then, if that's what you want. I thought you were better than that.'

'What does that mean?' I demand, my hands flying to my hips.

'Why can't you just be yourself, Lucy?' Kimmy says sadly.

'I *am* being myself – I've only changed my hair!' I protest, my pulse pounding in my ears. 'You just don't like it because now I'm more confident and popular and I'm finally fitting in!'

'Why would you *want* to fit in with *them*?'

'The most popular girls in our year?' I laugh. 'Like, duh!'

'*Like, duh!*' she mocks, pacing back and forth angrily. 'You even *sound* like them! Why do you want to be like them? They're horrible!'

'No, they're not!' I argue. 'They've been lovely tonight. *You're* the only one being horrible, and you're supposed to be my best friend!'

'And you're supposed to be mine!' Kimmy rounds on me, her eyes glistening like wet pebbles. 'But best friends don't break their promises!' Her voice cracks and she turns away from me. 'We were going to get our ears pierced together, remember? When we're thirteen? We had a deal!'

OMG, I totally forgot! Guilt prickles under my skin, but I'm too upset to apologize. 'Well . . . well, I'd probably *never* have got them pierced if I waited for you,' I retort. 'I never see you outside of school! You never have time for me any more – you're always too busy with your stupid sports! Like tonight!'

Kimmy throws up her hands. 'I had netball – we've got a match tomorrow!'

'Well, maybe you should go home and practise then!' I yell, storming out of the kitchen and slamming the door behind me.

'Material Girl' is just finishing and everyone else is giggling and laughing. Why does Kimmy have to take everything so seriously? I was having fun until she turned up! Then 'Holiday' comes on, and I feel a pang. Usually this would start an instant goof-off contest between us.

'Woo-hoo! This one's my favourite!' Shazza squeals. 'Come on, girls!' She swings her hips and waves her arms in the air, in perfect time with Madonna on the TV.

Freya laughs. 'Your mum is so cool!'

She wouldn't have said that if she'd met her two days ago!

I smile as I fall into step with the group, and as we twirl and kick and clap and giggle together I've never felt so popular in my life. Why should I let Kimmy spoil everything?

Suddenly the doorbell rings. 'Pizza!' Shazza cries, racing to the door.

Then, over the music, I hear a voice sing, 'Hollanda-aise!'

I turn to see Kimmy, arms and legs whirling like a Catherine wheel, her hair flying everywhere as she shakes her head wildly. 'Saliva-ate!'

A small smile plays at my lips.

'What is she doing?' Megan pulls a face as if she's smelled something gross.

I know exactly what she's doing. She's goofball-dancing, just like we always do.

'Those aren't the moves!' Viv says with a frown.

'She's so weird!' Nicole sneers.

Kimmy pretends to cram food in her mouth as she bounces up and down. *It would ta-aste . . . it would taste SO GOOD!*

'Uh, those aren't even the lyrics, Chung.' Megan smirks. 'Like, *duh!*'

'I know!' Kimmy laughs. 'That's the point, right, Luce?'

Everyone turns to stare at me and I feel my cheeks grow hot. #Cringe! How has the best night of my life suddenly become the most awkward? I look around for Shazza, but she's still outside.

What should I do? Should I join in with Kimmy and embarrass myself in front of the Megababes, just after I've *finally* been accepted? Or – wait . . . is that what Kimmy *wants*? My stomach hardens. Well, she can look like a fool by herself.

'I've no idea what she's doing. Weird!' I shrug.

'*Mega*-weird!' Megan sniggers, slipping her arm through mine. The rest of the Megababes laugh, but all I can see is the surprise and disappointment on Kimmy's face as she stops dancing. Then she runs out the door.

OMG. What have I done?

28 SHAZZA

'Keep the change – *Oof!*' Someone hurtles into my back, knocking me straight into the delivery guy! Pizza boxes crash everywhere as we both stumble. Then I look up and spot Kimmy racing away. What's going on?

I gather up the boxes, then go back into the lounge and dish them out – but there's no sign of Lucy. Uh-oh.

'Pizza!' I cry, opening the kitchen door to find her slumped miserably at the table.

'I'm not hungry,' she mutters.

'What *happened*?' I hurry over, sliding the pizza box on to the table as I sit down beside her. 'One minute everyone's totally psyched, dancing around, the next Kimmy's bowling me over as she rushes out the door! Did you two fight?'

'Kind of.' She explains what happened. 'I wanted to go after her, but I couldn't leave my own party!' Lucy sighs. 'Why can't we just all be friends together?'

'Ugh,' I groan, opening the pizza box and serving us each a big slice. 'I went through, like, the exact same thing last month. Me and my best friend Lily had a big bust-up when this new girl, Caroline, started at our school. I got jealous because they started going to ballet class together. But now we're all friends!' I beam, taking a bite of pizza.

99

'Really?' Lucy picks at her slice doubtfully, making a little pile of sweetcorn on her napkin.

'Mm-hmm.' I swallow. 'I was worried Caroline was going to, like, take my place, but I was being totally dumb. Just because you make new friends or like different things –' I pop a piece of Lucy's discarded sweetcorn in my mouth and grin – 'doesn't mean you can't still be best friends.'

Lucy smiles and passes me the rest of her sweetcorn.

'Just let Kimmy cool off, then talk to her later,' I advise. 'Ooh – and take her some cold pizza as a peace offering!'

'Cold pizza?' Lucy winces. 'Yuck!'

'Are you kidding? I LOVE cold pizza!'

'Weirdo!' She laughs, taking a big bite.

'Takes one to know one!' I wink. At least Lucy's smiling – and eating! – again.

Suddenly Megan rushes into the kitchen followed by the Mega-clones. 'Luce! Shazza! Quick!' she cries, her face pale. '*MEGA-emergency!*'

Lucy drops her pizza and jumps up. 'What's happened?!'

'Like, duh! Look at me!' Megan gestures to her school dress, which has the tiniest bit of pizza sauce smeared down the front. 'Help!'

That's the emergency?

'Don't worry!' Lucy says. 'I'm sure it'll come out.'

'Can you wash it for me, please, Shazza?' Megan asks anxiously.

'Um. Yeah . . . probably,' I say with a shrug.

'Thank you!' Megan beams. 'Luce, can I borrow something to wear?'

They hurry out, leaving me staring helplessly round the kitchen. I have no idea how to use a washing machine – especially a futuristic one! – and where on earth even *is* it?

'Oh, Luce, what an adorable room!' Megan coos as the Megababes follow me inside. 'Now, let's see what we've got here . . .'

She flings open my wardrobe doors and I wince. I *so* don't have anything cool enough for Megan to wear. This is going to be uber-embarrassing – especially if anyone spots Zebby! I shove him under my duvet quickly, but luckily the Megababes are too busy rifling through the hangers to notice. #CloseShave. But as Megan tosses an array of tops, jumpers and dresses into a mounting reject heap on my bed it's hard to resist the urge to crawl underneath and hide with him.

'What's this?' Megan says suddenly, peering inside a shopping bag.

I freeze as she pulls out the sparkly white dress Shazza bought me.

'Isn't that the one you tried on yesterday, Megan?' Cara says.

'When did you get this?' Megan asks, her voice sugary sweet.

'Um . . . it's new,' I gulp, feeling all the blood drain from my face.

'Obvs!' She pulls the receipt out of the bag. 'Yesterday afternoon. Four o'clock.'

Viv gasps. 'But that's just after you tried it on, Megan!'

'OMG, were you *spying* on us, Lucy?' Nicole rounds on me.

'No! I—'

'Lucy wouldn't do that, would you, Luce?' Megan says lightly. 'You wouldn't watch me try on a dress for the ball and then buy it yourself, *would you*?'

'No! I didn't even—'

'Because you'd know we can't *both* wear it, right?' Megan walks towards me, the expensive dress dangling from her fingertips. 'That'd be MEGA-lame. For both of us.' She smiles icily.

'Right,' I mumble, my cheeks burning.

She steps closer. 'So . . . who gets to wear it to the ball?'

'You should, Megan – you saw it first!' Cara says.

'And you looked so good in it, Megan!' Viv says quickly.

'So much better than Lucy would,' Nicole adds. 'No offence.'

Yeah, right.

'Now, girls –' Megan smiles – 'there's only *one* way to decide.' She tosses the dress to me. 'Put it on, Luce.'

'What?' I shake my head quickly. 'No!'

'Come on, we just want to see who wears it best – like in the magazines!'

'No!' I back away from them, my legs trembling. 'I

don't want to!' I fall backwards on to the bed, surrounded by all my rejected clothes.

'But, Lucy –' Megan tilts her head to one side as she looks down at me – 'how will we know who looks best in it?'

'You will,' I mutter, desperate for the humiliation to end.

'Sorry?' She leans closer, a hand to her ear.

'You'll look better in it,' I say, swallowing hard, desperately struggling not to cry. 'You look better in everything.'

Megan beams. 'Aw, that's so *sweet* of you, Lucy! Isn't it, babes?'

The Megababes smirk.

'So you won't mind if I borrow it, right?' Megan plucks the dress from my hands.

I look up. 'What?'

'Well, you see, I was going to buy this dress too . . . but now we've agreed we can't *both* wear it to the ball, that seems an *eensy* bit wasteful, doesn't it? I mean there's no point it just sitting in your wardrobe, right?' Megan steps back and flicks her hair triumphantly. 'In fact I could take it now, while I'm here! I do need to change out of my dirty dress, and you *did* say I could borrow your clothes . . .'

I sigh heavily, utterly beaten. 'Fine,' I mumble, my

eyes stinging as I glare at the floor, wishing it would just swallow me up.

'Great!' Megan squeals.

'Lucy!' Shazza calls, poking her head round the door. 'Could you put some more music on in the lounge, please? Megan, sweetie, the sooner I wash your dress, the more likely that stain will come out.'

'Just a minute, Shazza!' Megan smiles. 'I'm just gonna get changed. Lucy's loaned me the most beautiful dress. She's SUCH a great friend.'

'Takes one to know one!' Shazza says, winking at me.

If only she'd been here five minutes ago.

30 SHAZZA

Ugh! What a mega-mean, mega-bogus mega-jerk Megan is! I wanted to storm in five minutes ago when I overheard them being majorly nasty to poor Lucy, but then I had a *much* better idea . . .

I wait until Megan's changed, then give it ten minutes before heading into the lounge to find her flouncing around in Lucy's beautiful new dress, her clones cooing around her while Luce watches miserably from the corner.

I plaster on a sickly-sweet smile. 'OK, everyone, the limo's ready to take you home!' There's a chorus of groans, but Lucy looks relieved. 'Thanks for coming!' I call as the girls gather their bags and coats. 'Take care now.'

'Thanks, Shazza!' Megan cries as the others collect their things. 'It's been mega-cool!'

'Oh, you're welcome,' I call loudly. 'And I'll do my best to get the pizza sauce out of your dress – and that other stain too.' I wink at her.

Megan frowns. 'What other stain?'

I glance round quickly to make sure everyone's listening.

'You know, where you had your little –' I speak in a loud stage whisper – 'accident.'

Megan's jaw drops as a hush falls over the room.

'Don't worry, sweetie.' I pat her shoulder in my best

106

motherly manner. 'Everyone gets a little *over-excited* at parties sometimes, and occasionally, well, we don't get to the toilet in time, do we?'

There's a collective gasp and one of the girls snorts with laughter.

'What? No! I didn't *wet myself*!' Megan protests.

'It's absolutely nothing to be *embarrassed* about.' I smile. 'These things happen. Not that it's ever happened to Lucy, but I've heard it's a perfectly normal part of growing up for many girls.' I glance at Lucy, who is grinning from ear to ear.

'I swear! I didn't wet myself!' Megan's face has gone pinker than the limousine. She looks round at everyone, panic in her eyes as they giggle at her. '*I didn't!*' she yells. 'Someone must've set me up!'

'Now, Megan, really, who would do such a thing?' I reason. 'Besides, everyone's been in the lounge together, except you and your BFFs . . .'

Megan rounds on her clones, doubt and fear flickering across her face.

'There was no need to "accidentally" spill pizza sauce on your dress to get me to wash it,' I continue. 'If you'd just told the truth in the beginning, there'd only be one stain now, not two.'

The giggles grow louder, and I find it hard to keep a straight face as Megan opens and closes her mouth like a beached goldfish. This is so much fun! 'Hurry along, everyone. The limo's waiting. And be careful in Lucy's dress, now, won't you, Megan? That's dry-clean only.'

Everyone bursts out laughing as they scuttle outside, Megan following, red-faced. Lucy and I wave them off, then close the door and high-five.

'You –' Lucy grins at me – 'are UBER-AMAZING! Did you see Megan's face? She's *never* gonna live that down!'

'I thought Megan *liked* wee games?' I wink.

Lucy laughs and I beam back at her. She looks so much happier, plus she's stopped trying to be part of the Barbie-doll clique. Mission accomplished!

But will it be enough to de-stress Sharon?

31 LUCY

'Wow!' I say when Shazza *finally* sits me down in the lounge and fills me in on what she's learned about her amnesia. 'So *that's* why you're still here!' I guess I knew deep down it couldn't really be magic . . . but now I'm feeling worried – and more than a little guilty. I mean, I knew Mum was stressed out – but could I have prevented this? If we hadn't had that big argument on Sunday, would she have lost her memory?

'And you really think Mum's stressed out about *me*?' I ask Shazza.

'What else could it be?' She shrugs from her perch on the arm of the sofa. 'Her life seems pretty cool to me – lovely house, good job, great husband . . .'

I feel another stab of guilt.

'. . . nice-*ish* daughter!'

'Hey!' I nudge her.

'Just kidding,' Shazza laughs. 'So come on then, what else can I do to make you happy? I'm your fairy godmother, remember?'

'Well . . . Zak's finally noticed me and I've discovered Megan's not worth being friends with,' I begin, 'but I really need to fix things with Kimmy.'

'You can borrow my magic wand if you like.' Shazza grins, handing me the phone.

*

As soon as Kimmy picks up I apologize for not joining in with her goofy dance, and she apologizes for calling me a bimbo. Then I tell her about Megan and she nearly wets herself laughing! #Ironic

That's one of the things I love about Kimmy. Make her laugh, and all's forgiven.

'I can't believe your mum *did* that!' she giggles. 'You're right, she has changed – she's amazing!'

I grin.

'But you know, if you are worried about her, I could always ask my dad to pop round?'

'Well . . .' I open my mouth to tell her everything, then suddenly stop myself. Kimmy's dad is a psychotherapist for social services . . . If they find out my mother has the mind of a twelve-year-old, who knows what they'll do?

They might take her away. They might take *me* away. They might send me to live with Dad and Irritating Ingrid!

'Actually no, Mum's fine,' I fib. 'I think your dad was right, she's just getting over the divorce. You know, reinventing herself.'

'I thought so,' Kimmy says. 'See. Nothing to worry about!'

Nothing I can talk to Kimmy about anyway. Not till Mum's back to normal.

*

'Sorted?' Shazza asks hopefully as I hang up.

'Sorted.' I smile.

'Awesome!' She jumps up and takes a bow. 'Then my work here is done. Old-Shazza, I mean, *Sharon*, should be back by the morning! Which means we'd better make the most of tonight! Come on – I want to learn *all* the Just Dance moves!'

'OK!' I smile, but guilt still niggles in my stomach. If stress is what caused Mum's memory loss, was it really about me? Or was it – more likely – about Dad moving in with Irritating Ingrid? Something Shazza knows nothing about!

Should I tell her?

#Dilemma

'Lucy, *come on!*' Shazza cries, tossing me the Wii controller. 'So many dance moves, *so little time!*'

'All right!' I laugh, glancing at the clock as I join her. It is late – and it's not as if there's anything we can do about Dad, not tonight anyway. Besides, maybe Shazza's right. Maybe Mum *was* just stressed out about me, and now I'm happy, everything will go back to normal?

I guess we'll find out in the morning.

WEDNESDAY

32 SHAZZA

'Lucy! Wake up!' I shake her awake. 'It's Wednesday and I'm still here!'

'Huh? Shazza?'

'Yes!' I flop down on her bed. 'It's *me*! Not that I, like, don't, like, *like* being here, but —'

'There were far too many *likes* in that sentence,' Lucy moans. She is SO not a morning person.

'But it means you're still not happy!' I accuse her. 'How do we fix this?'

'Shazza, I'm fine. Honestly.' Lucy yawns, rubbing the sleep from her eyes. 'Zak even added me as a friend on TeenSpace last night and sent me a link to the new Star-Gazers single. I'm happy!'

'Then why am I still here?' I frown. 'Why was Sharon so stressed out?'

Lucy grimaces and pulls the duvet over her head.

'Come on! We have to look for *clues*!'

'Later!' she grumbles.

'Fine. *I'll* look.' I jump off the bed. But where? What would Nancy Drew do? Suddenly I snap my fingers. 'Lucy!' I rip the covers off her and she groans. 'Where's Sharon's Filofax? There's bound to be a clue in there!'

'Her *what*?' Lucy squints up at me.

'You know – her organizer, her diary, her contacts!'

'You mean her *phone*? It's all on there.'

'Really?' I gasp. 'Rad! So where on earth is it?' I hurry into the lounge, but the room's a total bombsite, with empty pizza boxes and sweet wrappers strewn everywhere, and there's no sign of the dinky phone. Suddenly it starts ringing and a pizza box shudders – awesome! It's like the phone *knew* I was searching for it! Is it *psychic*? I dig it out and stare at the screen in surprise.

'*Lucy?*'

'What?' She stumbles in, holding her mobile as she pulls on her school uniform. 'Why didn't you tell me what time it was? Kimmy'll be here soon!'

'Sorry – but why are you calling me?' I ask, confused.

'To help you find your phone, numpty.' Lucy yawns, hanging up.

'Genius!' I cry. 'So how do I find Sharon's diary?'

Lucy takes the mobile and jabs at it. 'OMG, you've got five voicemails and six texts!'

'Huh?' It's like she's speaking a foreign language.

'Lots of messages,' she explains. 'Wait – who's Sam?'

I shrug. 'As if *I'd* know! Duh!'

Lucy shows me the screen.

Sam: Are we still on for tonight?

'No way!' I cry. 'I can't meet someone I don't even know! Unless . . . d'you think he might know why Sharon's so stressed out?'

'Too risky.' Lucy shakes her head. 'I'll tell him no.' Her fingers fly over the screen.

'Wait!' I cry. 'You've got to show me how to do that!'

It takes a while to get the hang of 'texting', especially when the bogus machine keeps guessing what I'm thinking — wrongly! But finally I manage to text Sam, whoever he is, to say I'm not well.

'What now?' I ask. 'We have to find out what Sharon's problem is.'

Lucy takes a deep breath. 'Listen —'

Suddenly the doorbell rings and she jumps up. 'That'll be Kimmy! I've gotta go!'

'But we have to find clues!' I protest, hurrying after her.

'We will —' she nods, shoving books into her backpack — 'but I have to go to school! No one's going to believe I'm ill again after having a party last night!'

'True.' My heart sinks. 'If only Detective Dan was

here – he's great at working out puzzles and always guesses the end of mysteries. That's it!' I cry. 'Let's call him!'

'No!' Lucy says quickly. 'We can't – we're not allowed to ring Dad on business trips cos he's uber-busy and it's uber-expensive. But I'll get home as soon as I can after school and we'll look for clues then, I promise.'

I sigh. 'Pinky promise?'

'Course.' Lucy shakes my little finger, hugs me, then hurries out of the room, leaving me feeling as lost and clueless as ever.

33 LUCY

Saved by the bell! I grab my coat and scarf, feeling guiltier than ever for not telling Shazza the truth about Dad. After all, I'm sure Kimmy was right: Mum's strange behaviour *must* be caused by stress about the divorce – but I can't drop a bombshell like that and then rush off to school, can I? I'll tell her as soon as I get home, when I've got time to explain everything properly.

'Hi!' Kimmy beams as I open the door.

'Hi!' I hug her. I'm so glad our fight is over.

'So, come on! Tell me everything!' Her eyes gleam as we start walking. 'I want a complete blow-by-blow re-enactment. What did Megan say? What did she do? Did the Megabimbos stick up for her? Or were they too embarrassed?'

'Shh!' I hiss as I spot them just ahead. Or rather, *most* of them . . . 'Weird. Where's Megan?' I whisper, seeing only Nicole, Cara and Viv. 'I don't think I've ever seen the Megababes without her.'

'You mean they're not *actually* joined at the hip?' Kimmy gasps. 'It's a medical miracle!'

I laugh and she grins back. 'So come on! Re-enactment! Now!' she demands.

I tell Kimmy all about it as we walk to school. Then, as we arrive, a group of girls from the year below races up to us. 'Lucy, is it *true*?' one asks, her eyes lit up with excitement. 'Did Megan really *wet herself* at your party?'

I frown. 'How did you know?'

'She *did*!' The girls giggle. 'OMG! That's, like, the best gossip *ever*!'

'Are you talking about Megan?' a lanky boy from the year above asks.

'Who else?' says a short boy with a cruel smirk. 'Everybody's talking about it!'

Sure enough, suddenly I find myself in the middle of a squealing crowd.

'You should've seen Megan's face!'

'It was utterly priceless!'

'I can't believe she *deliberately* got pizza sauce on her dress to cover it up!'

'Lame.'

'*So* lame!'

'So *embarrassing*!'

'*MEGA*-embarrassing!'

'She will *never* live this down!'

'I'll never forget what your mum said, Lucy!' Freya laughs. '"*Don't worry, sweetie, everyone gets a little over-excited at parties sometimes!*"'

'Did you bring her dress to school today?' Iris from my class asks.

'Um, no . . . I forgot,' I fib. Shazza and I still can't figure out how to work the washing machine. #DomesticFail

'Uh-oh! She'll have to be careful not to get too *excited* today then – otherwise she might run out of school dresses!' someone else quips.

Everyone bursts out laughing, but I start to feel a bit sick. 'Maybe I should tell the truth?' I whisper to Kimmy.

'No way,' she hisses back. 'Megan's just getting a taste of her own medicine. Besides, you know what gossip's like. It won't last long.'

'I'm SO glad it was Megan!' Freya cries.

'Me too!' Iris agrees. 'She's always making fun of my braces.'

'And my lithp,' adds a girl I don't know.

'And my clumsiness . . . ouch!' yelps a boy, stubbing his toe and hobbling away.

I smile. Maybe Kimmy's right, Megan does deserve it. She's spent years being mean to everyone else. She should know how it feels!

But as the day goes by I feel less sure. Megan sits by herself in every lesson. Even the Megababes keep as far away from her as possible, choosing a table on the opposite side of the room.

'Have they fallen out?' I ask Freya during English.

'I think they're trying to distance themselves from the embarrassment,' she whispers.

'Really?' My stomach lurches. 'Wow.'

'Lucy?' Ms Banks points a whiteboard marker at me. 'Do you have something you'd like to say to the class?'

Everyone turns to stare at me.

'Um, no, miss,' I mutter, feeling my cheeks burn.

'Well, maybe you could read out your short story for us then.' She folds her arms.

I freeze. 'What story?'

Ms Banks's face falls. 'The short story I set for homework yesterday?'

'Um . . . sorry, I guess I forgot it.' I wonder if amnesia's contagious?

Ms Banks's braids swish as she shakes her head. 'Then I guess I'll be seeing you in after-school detention tomorrow. You know the rules.'

Yep. What goes around comes around – and bites you on the bum. #Karma

34 SHAZZA

Ugh. How can *anyone's* diary be so BORING! And how majorly depressing that it's MINE! I was so psyched when I found the tiny book, but I can't believe it's just filled with dreary appointments – and no clues at all! I toss it on to the floor in disgust, along with the rest of the useless contents of Sharon's handbag, and bury my head in a cushion in despair.

Then I hear it.

Something's singing.

And buzzing.

OMGA, it's the dinky singing phone!

I look around blindly. Where did I put it? I listen carefully, picking my way through the debris as I follow the sound like a dog chasing a scent. The noise is definitely loudest in the kitchen – but WHERE IS IT? Argh! Why do they make them so *tiny*?

Finally I spot it under a chair, buzzing and jumping around like an angry insect. *Lucy's School* is written on the screen.

Uh-oh.

Holy guacamole, I *have* to answer it! What if something's happened to Lucy? I pick it up and jab at it until it stops ringing.

'Hello?' a woman says.

'Hello?' I say quickly. 'Is everything OK? Is Lucy all right?'

'Lucy's fine.'

'Phew!'

'But she's got an after-school detention tomorrow.'

'Oh. Right. OK!' I say, too anxious about slipping up to even pretend to be angry.

The woman sighs. 'I'm sorry, it's school policy.'

She's *apologizing* for giving Lucy detention? Her teachers are so nice!

'It's fine. Thanks for letting me know—'

'Are you OK?' she interrupts before I can work out how to hang up.

'Yes,' I say quickly. 'Why?'

'I thought you were ill?'

'Oh yes! I am!' I kick myself. I totally forgot I'm supposed to be off work, sick. *Doofus!* 'I mean, *ATISHOO*, I'm not feeling well at *all* actually. In fact, I've really gotta go! Bye!'

I manage to jab the 'off' button before I can make her any more suspicious. Ugh! Pretending to be Sharon is majorly hard work!

35 LUCY

'At last!' Shazza cries, rushing to meet me as soon as I open the front door.

'Sorry!' I pant. 'I hurried home as fast as I could!' Not that I'd *recognize* my usually uber-tidy house as home any more – the discarded pizza boxes are still scattered over the floor, which somehow seems to have accumulated even *more* mess, and the whole lounge looks like a tornado has hit it.

'I can't find ANY clues about why Sharon's stressed out!' Shazza wails, her curly hair frizzier than ever. 'What are we going to *do*?'

'Listen, Shazza . . .' I say slowly, taking a deep breath. 'There's something I need to tell you.'

'What?' Her eyes light up. 'Have you figured it out?'

'I . . . well . . .' *This is it. I can do this . . .*

Suddenly the doorbell rings.

'Not *again*!' Shazza moans. 'Ignore it!' she begs as I hurry to the window.

But I can't. It's Dad!

'Who is it?' Shazza frowns, peering over my shoulder.

My heart beats fast. Should I lie? Stall for time? Pretend we're not in? What's Dad *doing* here? And why didn't I tell Shazza the truth when I had the chance?!

'Lucy!' he calls, ringing the bell again. 'Sweetheart, are you ready?'

'Holy guacamole!' Shazza gasps. 'Is that *Danny*?'

I swallow hard. 'Yes, but—'

'AWESOME!' she squeals, racing to the door. 'Detective Dan will figure this out in no time!'

'Wait!' I hurry after her. 'Shazza, STOP!'

But I'm too late.

Shazza flings open the front door and Dad's face turns white with shock.

'Sharon?' he frowns. 'You look . . . different.'

'So do you!' she exclaims. 'You've got so . . . so *hairy*!'

He stares at her as if she's an alien.

'Sha— Mum, I need to talk to you.' I grab her arm and try to pull her back inside.

'Lucy, what's happened to your *hair*?' Dad cries. 'Is it *permanent*?!'

'Um . . .'

'It looks gorgeous, Lucy!' My stomach tightens at the sound of the familiar Aussie twang. What's *she* doing here? 'Are you ready to go?' she calls out the window of Dad's car.

I frown. 'Go where?'

'Chez Charlotte.' Dad glares at Shazza. 'I spoke to your mother about it on Sunday. Didn't she tell you?'

Shazza looks at him blankly. 'Sorry, I must have . . . forgotten!'

'Well, we've got a table booked in twenty minutes!' Dad glances at his watch.

'Awesome!' Shazza grins. 'I'll just grab—'

'I'll get my stuff!' I interrupt, dragging Shazza back inside. 'Just give me five minutes, OK, Dad?' I say, slamming the door.

'Chez Charlotte sounds very fancy!' Shazza gushes. 'Will I be OK in these pink jeg-legging-things, or should I get changed?'

'No, listen, Shazza—'

'I'll get changed.' She nods.

'Wait!' I block her way. 'There's something I need to tell you. About Dad.'

'I can't believe how much he's changed!' Shazza exclaims. 'I mean, *obviously* he's changed – it's been, like, over thirty years!'

'Shazza—'

'But you can still totally tell he's Danny, because he has those same twinkly green eyes – but he's got so OLD and TALL – and I can't believe he's got a *beard*! I can't believe I married Danny Andrews! *I can't believe I'm married at all!*'

'You're *not*!' I cry.

Shazza's smile slips slowly from her face. 'What?'

#Crumpets. It wasn't meant to come out like that. If only she'd *listen*!

'What do you mean?' Her voice trembles. 'I saw the wedding photos . . .'

'I know, but . . .'

'But . . . what?' she whispers.

I take her hand. 'Shazza,' I say, as gently as I can, 'you're divorced.'

36 SHAZZA

The word hits me like a bucket of icy water. '*Divorced?*'

'I'm sorry,' Lucy sighs, squeezing my hand. 'I didn't want to tell you like that.'

'Wow!' I feel dizzy.

'Here, sit down.' She helps me to the sofa and I sink into it, my head spinning.

'H-how long have we been divorced?' My eyes prickle.

'About six months,' Lucy says softly.

I swallow. 'So . . . Danny wasn't on a business trip?'

She shakes her head. 'He doesn't live here any more.'

That's why he didn't use a key. Duh.

I frown at Lucy. 'Why did you *lie* to me? I thought we could tell each other anything?'

She sags down beside me. 'I didn't want to upset you. I-I thought you were only here for a day! And then it was too late and—'

'This is my *life*, Lucy,' I snap, flinching away from her, my face flushing with humiliation. 'I have a right to know if I'm married or not! I feel like such a doofus!'

'I'm *sorry*!'

The doorbell rings again. 'You'd better go,' I mutter. 'You'll be late.'

'No – Shazza, I can't leave –' She touches my

shoulder but I shrug her off. 'You must have so many questions . . .'

Like, a million.

'What happened?' I sniff. 'What went wrong? Why did we split up?'

She shakes her head. 'I don't know. But . . .'

'But what?' I demand.

Lucy squirms. 'Well. Dad got together with Ingrid pretty quickly, so . . .'

'Who's Ingrid?' I frown. 'Wait, that *Australian girl*?'

Lucy nods slowly.

I stare at her. 'They're *dating*?'

She winces. 'They're, er, living together.'

'Holy guacamole, Lucy!' I jump up and start pacing the room. 'What *else* have you been hiding from me?'

'Nothing! I swear!' Lucy looks as if she's about to burst into tears.

'So not only am I *not* married happily ever after, I'm divorced and my ex-husband is dating some surfer chick straight off *Neighbours*!' I kick a pizza box hard and it tumbles across the room, spilling its greasy contents over the carpet.

'Shazza—'

'I *asked* you if there was anything else that could've been stressing Sharon out!' I round on her. 'And you just . . . you totally lied to my face!'

'I'm sorry!' Lucy wails, staring miserably at her feet.

'No *wonder* Sharon was stressed!' I shake my head, everything suddenly making sense.

The doorbell rings again, for longer this time. 'Lucy!' Danny calls. 'We'll lose our table!'

'Go,' I tell her.

'No, Shazza—'

'*Go!*' I fling the lounge door open so hard it slams against the wall, startling us both. 'I need some space.' I turn away from her, hugging my arms.

'Lucy!' Danny calls again.

She sighs. 'I'll be back as soon as I can, and I've got my phone if you . . . if you need me.'

I nod. But I still can't look at her.

'I'm sorry,' she whispers.

I close my eyes, listening to her footsteps as she walks away. The front door clicks shut, then gravel crunches as they drive off.

Then I crumple on to the sofa and cry my eyes out.

37 LUCY

I wish I'd told Shazza about the divorce before. And I wish *Mum'd* told *me* how stressed she was, instead of bottling it all up and pretending everything was fine. Maybe if we'd talked more, she wouldn't have got so stressed out she lost her memory?

I check my phone again, but Shazza still hasn't replied to any of my texts.

I don't blame her.

'I really like your earrings, Lucy.' Ingrid beams, turning in the passenger seat. 'Very chic.'

'Uh, thanks. Mum bought them for me,' I mumble.

'Are they *pierced*?' Dad splutters. 'I thought you had to wait until you're thirteen?'

I shrug and look out of the window. 'Mum changed her mind.'

'That's not all she's changed!' Ingrid cries, her eyes sparkling. 'She looks so . . . *striking*!'

I glare at her.

'Is your mum all right?' Dad's eyes meet mine in the rear-view mirror. 'She didn't seem quite herself.'

I hesitate. *Should I tell him the truth?* After all, maybe if I explain how secretly upset Mum is about the divorce, they'll get back together and that'll fix everything.

'Actually she's been off work this week,' I begin.

'I'm sorry to hear that.' Dad frowns. 'Maybe that's why she hasn't returned any of my calls.'

'That's probably why she forgot about dinner today too,' Ingrid adds.

I grit my teeth. She *did* forget! That and everything else from the last three decades!

'Well, we made it in time, and the three of us are going to have a lovely meal together.' Dad smiles as we pull into the car park. 'That's all that matters.'

The three of us. Ugh! If Mum and Dad are going to get back together, I'll have to get Ingrid out of the way first . . .

Operation Break-Up is on.

38 SHAZZA

I have never felt so lonely in my entire life. Sitting here on an unfamiliar sofa, in an unfamiliar house, in an unfamiliar time, everything just feels so WRONG. I find Zebby and hug him tight, breathing in his comforting smell — the only familiar thing in this entire world.

Except Lucy. She's the only person I know here, and the only person who understands what's happened to me. But she's the last person I want to talk to. She lied to me. She treated me like a child, not her friend. Especially not like her mother.

Mother.

My throat swells. I miss Ma and Pa so much. What if I never see them again?

But wait — maybe I *can* see them! I've only travelled forward a few decades after all; maybe they're still around, still at the same address.

I grab the phone and quickly dial the one number I know off by heart, then cross my fingers tight.

'Hello,' a familiar voice says.

'Ma!' I cry, my heart leaping. 'Ma, it's me!'

'You have reached the phone of Sheila and Alfred Miller.'

My heart plummets. It's just the — what's-its-name — *voicemail.*

'Please leave your message after the tone.'

I hang up. I can't explain what's happened on a machine! I need to see them. I need a hug! I need Ma to make everything better, like she always does.

I need to go home.

39 LUCY

I need to get rid of Ingrid.

'Do you have something in your teeth?' I ask her as we sit down, hoping she'll go to the loos to check.

'Gosh, how embarrassing! Thanks, Lucy!' She pulls a compact mirror from her handbag and my heart sinks. 'I can't see anything . . .'

#Fail

'Are you ready to order?' the waiter asks, hurrying over.

'Goodness, I haven't even read the menu yet!' Dad says.

'You don't need to!' I quip. 'You always have steak and chips!'

Dad laughs. 'I do love a good steak!'

'How about *salmon* steak instead?' Ingrid interjects. 'Much healthier, and just as tasty!'

'Sounds good,' Dad says with a sigh.

'But you *always* have steak and chips!' I gasp. I can't believe he's going to let *her* choose for him! #Irritating

'I'll have the same.' Ingrid beams at the waiter. 'What about you, Lucy? Shall we make it salmon all round?'

I scan the menu quickly. 'I'll have the double-decker gourmet cheeseburger and chunky chips, please,' I tell the waiter. 'With extra bacon, cheese and onion rings.'

I shoot Ingrid a triumphant look. She might have Dad under her thumb, but not me.

'Oh to be young!' Ingrid titters. 'You can eat anything at your age, you're so lucky!'

'You're not *that* much older than me, Ingrid,' I reply, not missing a beat.

'Oh please, you flatter me!' Ingrid pats my hand and I snatch it away. That *so* wasn't the intention. #Uber-Irritating

'Actually, fish is great for keeping skin looking youthful,' Ingrid continues. 'I get my love of seafood from my father – he loves fishing. There's nothing like being out on the open sea, no one else for miles around.'

#Boring

'It sounds amazing.' Dad smiles. 'Why don't you show Lucy your photos?'

'Ooh! Good idea!' She pulls out her mobile, swipes at the screen a few times, and a picture of a tanned older man on a boat appears, the sun sparkling on the glittering sea beside him, a golden beach visible in the background. I have to admit, it does look beautiful.

'There's no place like Oz,' Ingrid declares.

My stomach tightens.

Then why doesn't she *go home*!

40 SHAZZA

There's no place like home. And I have never been so glad to get here! As the taxi pulls into my road I feel my whole body relax. Finally! This is the world I recognize.

I smile as I climb out of the cab and look up at my house. It might be a bit older, a little more worn around the edges, but it's still mine: the garden wall I sit on while I wait for Lily to walk to school with me; the welcome mat I've wiped my feet on a thousand times; the doorbell that plays that irritating tune Ma loves so much.

My heart beats loudly as I press it. I can't wait to see Ma and Pa again, but I'm nervous too. I wonder what they look like now. They'll be old . . . retired even.

I ring the doorbell again.

And again.

But they don't answer. There's no one home. Duh! They didn't answer the phone after all.

It's OK, I tell myself, swallowing my disappointment. It's getting late; they'll be back soon. I'll just let myself in and wait for them.

I feel under the mat for the spare key – but it's gone.

I'm locked out.

I'm locked out of my life.

My pulse quickens.

Breathe.

Maybe there's a window open round the back. Even if it's an upstairs window, I can always climb up the apple tree. I hurry around the side of the house. Then I freeze.

Oh my giddy aunt! It's gone!

All that's left of the tree is an ugly blunt stump. I sink down on to it, my heart aching. I loved that apple tree. It was my climbing frame, my shady reading spot, an endless source of summer snacks, my escape route . . . and now it's gone.

I feel like I've lost a friend.

I feel like I've lost myself.

41 LUCY

Finally she's gone! I almost jump for joy as Ingrid disappears to the loo after the main course – at last I have a chance to talk to Dad!

'I'm glad we've got a moment alone together,' he says.

'Me too.' I smile. 'We hardly ever get time one on one like this.'

'You're right – we don't see each other enough. That's what I want to talk to you about actually.' He takes my hand. 'The thing is . . . I think family is the most important thing in life.'

'Me too!' I beam. This is going so well! Maybe he wants to move back home after all.

'And I know Ingrid feels the same way.'

I blink. Huh?

'She's been really homesick lately,' Dad continues. 'She misses her family. She misses Australia.'

'I guess that's what happens when you move to the other side of the world.' #Duh

'Well . . . that's the thing.' Dad swallows. 'She wants to move back.'

'To *Australia*?' I stare at him as he nods, unable to believe my ears. Ingrid's *leaving*? This is *perfect*!

'I'm sorry,' I say, squeezing his hand and trying my best to sound sympathetic as my heart cartwheels with joy. 'I know you really like her.'

'We're . . . not breaking up.' He takes a deep breath. 'Ingrid's asked me to go with her.'

My heart crashes into a ditch. '*What?*'

'Lucy—'

'She wants you to move to *Sydney*?'

'Yes.'

I can't believe this! 'What did you *say*?'

'I . . . told her I'd think about it.'

'You're *thinking* about it?' I snatch my hand away. 'You were just saying we should see each other *more*!'

'Well, yes—'

'But that's gonna be a bit *tricky* if you're several thousand miles away, isn't it?' I exclaim. I can see people at nearby tables glaring at me, but I don't care if I'm making a scene!

'Well, that's . . . that's why I'd like you to come too,' Dad says hopefully. 'We both would. We'd love you to live with us. In Sydney.'

I stare at him like he's a complete stranger.

'You've always wanted to go to Australia—'

'Not to *live*!' I shriek.

'And Sydney's beautiful. You could go to the beach all the time, learn to surf . . .'

'But-but what about Mum?' I splutter.

His smile fades. 'Your mum's a big girl.'

I snort. If only he knew!

'She says it's up to you.'

'*What?*' I stare at him in shock. 'Mum *knows* about this?'

'Of course! I spoke to her about it on Sunday – that's why I arranged to have dinner with you tonight. So we could talk about it.'

OMG. 'You told her on *Sunday?*'

He nods.

Suddenly everything makes sense! Dad told Mum about wanting to move to Australia, and *the very next day* she woke up with amnesia? *That* must be the cause! She's stressed about Dad leaving . . . and the possibility of losing me too!

'Look,' Dad says gently, 'just think about it—'

'I don't have to!' I yell, shoving my chair back. 'How could you do this to me? To us!' I storm off to the toilets, unable to stand the sight of him for a moment longer.

'Lucy, are you OK?' Ingrid gasps as I race past her.

'Leave me alone!' I snap, running into a cubicle. I lock the door and collapse on to the lid of the toilet. *How could he make me choose between them?*

Not that there's any choice really. Even though Mum drives me up the wall, there's no way I'm leaving her – especially now she's lost her memory! But I can't tell Dad about Shazza either now, I realize miserably. He might decide I'm not safe living with her. He might even use it as an excuse to *make* me go to Australia! Then Shazza would be all alone, a twelve-year-old trapped in a middle-aged body – forever!

#Nightmare!

42 SHAZZA

This is a nightmare.

I trace the grainy whorls of the tree stump miserably, grieving for the dead apple tree, and for all the hopes and dreams I had. What happened to my *life*?

I squeeze my eyes shut and hot tears spill down my cheeks. I *wish* this was just a nightmare. That in the morning I could wake up back in 1985 and redo everything. I'd avoid Danny Andrews like the plague for a start . . . but then, I guess, Lucy wouldn't even exist.

Lucy.

I pull my mobile out of my pocket. Four missed calls and five texts – all from her.

Lucy: RU OK? xxxx

Huh? Who's RU? Oh! I get it. *Are you . . .*

Lucy: I'm SOOOO sorry xxx

Lucy: Please call me back xxxx

Lucy: I'm so sorry I didn't tell you – I didn't want to upset you. Am an idiot. xxxx

> **Lucy:** Miss U. Where RU? Tried calling U @ home.
> RU OK? Am worried & SOOO sorry. xxx

I sigh. I should call her back. After all, as angry as I am about her lying to me, I guess I understand why she did it. And it's not her fault my life's like this. She didn't make my mistakes. I did.

I just don't remember.

I feel like my entire life is one big surprise party, where everyone else knows what's going on and I'm groping around in the dark for the light switch, clueless and terrified of what's going to jump out at me next.

'Shazza?' a gruff voice says suddenly.

I leap off the tree stump, startled, and spot a tall figure leaning over the garden fence.

I wipe my eyes and back away nervously. 'Who's there?'

'It's me – Trev.'

'*Trev?*' I peer at him through the darkness. No *way*. He's so old! And BALD! His head gleams like an egg in the moonlight, and as I step closer I notice his beer belly hanging over his tracksuit trousers. That's *Trev?* My mullet-haired teenage heart-throb? What *happened?*

'I thought it was you,' Trev says, lighting a cigarette. 'I feel like a teenager again, hiding out here, but Mum doesn't let me smoke inside. "The curtains! Think of the curtains, Trevor!"' he mimics, and I find myself smiling. Trev's mum's always been majorly house-proud. She always makes me take my shoes off before I'm allowed in.

'Want one?' Trev holds up the cigarette packet.

I hesitate. I've never smoked in my life – well, not that I know of anyway. Maybe I *do* smoke in the future . . .

'OK.' I shrug, feeling reckless. 'Can you, um, light it for me?' I have no idea how to!

'Sure.' Trev lights another cigarette and passes it to me. I slide it carefully between my lips, tentatively inhale – then immediately start coughing! Why would *anyone* smoke? It's *TOTALLY GROSS*! I feel as if my throat's on fire!

'You OK?' Trev asks, startled.

'I just remembered that I quit,' I croak, my eyes streaming as I pass the cigarette back.

'Very smart,' he says, leaning forward to take it – and suddenly I smell the smoke on his breath, mixed with beer – and is that garlic? It's totally gross!

'I've been trying to give up for ages,' Trev confesses. 'You were always smarter than me. It's funny – I was just telling my daughter about us the other day.'

'Really?' I look around. Wow. Trev has a daughter too?

He nods. 'She's a teenager now, and wants to start dating, so I thought it'd help get the message through that it's cool to take things slowly, that she shouldn't let herself be pressured into anything she doesn't feel comfortable with. I liked the way you always stuck up for yourself.'

I smile.

'I know it probably didn't seem that way when I dumped you for Lara Thompson, but I did. I admired you.'

My heart stops. Trev *dumped* me? For *Lara Thompson*? The girl in the year above with the big boobs?

'She wasn't a patch on you by the way. Just older. I was such a jerk. My friends all told me, but I didn't listen.' He shakes his head and I'm glad it's dark, so he can't see the tears stinging my eyes. It's totally stupid – it was over thirty years ago, and I'm SO glad I didn't end up marrying bald, stinky, fat, middle-aged jerk Trev . . . but it hurts.

'I regretted it almost immediately,' Trev confesses. 'But there was no going back. I was too ashamed. I'm *still* ashamed.' He sighs. 'If only we could turn back time, eh?'

I bite my lip. *If only.*

'I was so wrong to pressure you – and you were totally right to want to take things slowly. I just hope my Jess would do the same. If I had my way, I wouldn't let any boys within three miles of her, but you can't watch your kids 24-7, can you? You used to sneak out of your bedroom window, remember?' He grins.

I nod.

'Y'know, my mum still gives me a hard time.' He winces. 'She blames my "bad influence" for you failing that big piano exam – she used to love listening to you play next door, and always says if I hadn't distracted you so much you could've been a concert pianist by now.'

I snort. 'I never wanted to be a pianist!'

'Phew!' Trev laughs. 'I figured that if you'd wanted it enough you'd have made it happen. "Your destiny is in your own hands." That's what you always said.'

I look up. That *is* what I always say . . .

'That's what I tell Jess too,' Trev continues. 'Of course, she just rolls her eyes at me. I don't know what's harder – being a teenager or parenting one, eh? Your Lucy's nearly the same age, isn't she?'

I nod. Then a sudden thought hits me.

OMGA! Is *this* why Sharon doesn't want Lucy to date Zak? Because she thinks older boys are jerks and that he'll end up breaking her heart and mucking up her schoolwork?

'Well, if she's anything like you, you must be very proud.' Trev smiles and stubs out his disgusting cigarette on the fence post. 'Good to see you, Shazza.'

'You too, Trev.' I smile back. Because he's totally right – *I'm* right! My destiny *is* in my own hands. Whatever's happened in the past, this is *my* life now.

And I'm going to fix it.

43 LUCY

I am SO going to fix this. I have to. After all, if I don't stop Dad going to Australia, Mum'll never get her memory back.

#NotAnOption

I splash cold water on my face, pull myself together, then head back to the table.

'Lucy!' Dad jumps up anxiously as I approach. 'I'm sorry, I shouldn't have just blurted everything out like that—'

'It's fine. I'm sorry. I overreacted,' I reply, forcing a smile as I take my seat.

Dad glances at Ingrid, then sits back down slowly. 'Are you sure?'

I nod. 'It was just . . . a shock, that's all. I need some time to think about it.'

'Of course!' Ingrid says, nervously fiddling with her napkin. 'There's still some time.'

I frown. 'How much time?'

Dad and Ingrid look at each other.

'Well . . .' Dad hesitates. 'I mean . . . Ingrid's been offered a job starting at the end of the month, but—'

My stomach tightens. 'The end of the *month*?'

'A vacancy's come up at my cousin's gym,' Ingrid explains. 'I just found out. That's what got me thinking about moving back home in the first place.'

Wow! Operation Break-Up now has a deadline. A very tight deadline.

Which means we have no time to lose.

I plaster a smile on my face. 'What are you guys doing tomorrow night?'

'I'm so sorry!' I cry, hugging Lucy the moment she opens the front door. 'I majorly overreacted!'

'No *I'm* sorry!' She squeezes me tightly. 'I should've told you the truth from the beginning. Are you OK?'

I nod. 'I am now.'

Suddenly Lucy wrinkles her nose. 'Is something burning?'

'My toast!' I hurry back to the kitchen to rescue my makeshift dinner. 'Ugh, that's the last of the bread too.' I groan. 'It's been one of those evenings.'

I tell Lucy all about going home and talking to Trev as I scrape the burnt crumbs into the bin.

'OMG,' Lucy says slowly. 'So *that's* why Mum doesn't want me to date Zak? But Zak's not like that.'

'I didn't think *Trev* was like that!' I counter, grabbing the margarine from the fridge.

'Wait.' Lucy jumps up and tosses me a jar of chocolate spread. 'This'll cover the burnt taste better – and you definitely deserve some comfort food! What an uber-rubbish night!'

'Actually . . . it's OK,' I say, coating my toast with chocolate. 'Trev made me realize that while I can't change my past, I can totally fix my future.' I take a large bite.

'You're right.' Lucy grabs Sharon's laptop from the kitchen counter. 'We just need to break Dad and Ingrid up. By the end of the month.'

'*What?*' I splutter, spraying toast crumbs everywhere.

Lucy fills me in on everything Danny told her at dinner, and I can't believe my ears. Not only does my bogus husband leave me for a younger woman, but now he wants to take my daughter away to the other side of the world?

'I told him I'd think about it,' Lucy says, opening the laptop.

'WHAT?' I almost choke on my toast this time. 'Lucy, you can't go!'

'As if!' she cries, tapping away. 'I just told him that to buy us some time to split them up.'

'But . . . how?'

'Here's how!' Lucy spins the laptop round to show me a picture of a fancy-looking swimming pool and lots of attractive people wearing bathrobes.

'Huh?'

'I asked Dad if I could have a spa date with Ingrid after school tomorrow to "get to know her better".' Lucy's eyes sparkle. 'He booked it there and then! Dad will be Ingrid-free for at least three hours, so he's going to come over here. I told him you wanted to talk to him about Australia, but really you're going to put him off Ingrid!'

'But *how*?' I stare at her. 'Luce, I don't know anything *about* Ingrid! And I can't spend an evening with Danny without him guessing I've got amnesia — I can't remember anything about *our entire marriage*!'

'Hmm.' Lucy frowns. 'That could be problematic.'

'Duh!' I cry.

'Don't worry. I'll fill you in.' She smiles. 'It'll be fine!'

Famous last words.

THURSDAY

45 LUCY

Shazza and I sit up late into the night prepping for Operation Break-Up. I tell her everything I know about her life as she makes revision cards. Next morning we're exhausted.

And panicking. One slip-up = disaster!

'OK.' I pick yet another card. 'Date you got married?'

'Ooh, I know this one – it was on the wedding album!' Shazza twirls her hair round her finger anxiously. 'Um . . . 23 July?'

'Nearly!' I wince. 'The twenty-seventh.'

'Argh!' She flops back on to the bed. 'How am I supposed to memorize an entire marriage by tonight? It's impossible!'

'No, it's not,' I soothe. 'You can do this, Shazza. I know you can. You have to.' I glance at the clock. 'And I have to get to school.'

'But I'm meant to go to the doctor's later,' Shazza whines. 'I don't even know where it is!'

Oh crumpets! I'd forgotten about that. 'I'll call and cancel the appointment,' I tell her. After all, if the doctor reports Shazza to social services, I'll definitely be sent to live with Dad. *In Australia.* 'Besides, we know what's wrong with you now,' I add reassuringly. 'And we know how to fix it.'

'Only if I manage to learn everything in time!' Shazza wails. 'This is, like, the hardest exam ever – only worse! There's so much more at stake!'

'You'll be fine!' I smile encouragingly, wishing I felt as confident as I sounded. 'Just keep rereading the revision cards. I'll get back from school as quickly as I can, and we can go through everything again before they arrive. OK?' I hug her tight. 'Good luck!'

She sighs. 'I'm gonna need it.'

We both are.

46 SHAZZA

Ugh! This is hopeless! I've been staring at these bogus cards all morning, desperately trying to memorize the facts and anecdotes, but *nothing* is going in! I need some brain food.

Food. Danny's favourite foods are . . . I try to remember as I walk to the kitchen: peanut butter, cheese-and-onion crisps and chicken-something-or-other . . . Chicken chasseur? Chicken supreme?

Argh! My mind is a total blank!

As is the fridge. A lonely tub of margarine and a half-empty bottle of stinky milk stare back at me, along with a packet of weird purple leaves (do we have a rabbit? Must check!) and a plastic tub of something green and sludgy-looking. I lift the lid tentatively, then recoil at the stench — Gross! No brain food here. I'll have to go to the super-duper-market if I actually want to eat anything today, let alone chicken . . . Kiev? Parmigiana?

I give up and look at the card. Chicken cacciatore!

I close my eyes and try to memorize it.

Danny's favourite meal is chicken cacciatore. Danny's favourite meal is chicken cacciatore. Danny's favourite meal is . . .

Suddenly I grin.

Danny's favourite meal is chicken cacciatore? Then I'll cook it for him tonight!

I find a recipe online, print it out, then grab Sharon's handbag and race out the door.

Genius!

47 LUCY

'Are you OK?' Kimmy frowns as she sits down next to me in maths. 'You've been really quiet all day.'

I bite my lip. I'm dying to tell her what's happened with Mum and all about Operation Break-Up, but because of her dad's job it's just too risky.

'I'm fine,' I fib, flashing her a weak smile. 'Just tired.'

'Don't lie to me,' Kimmy says tightly. 'I'm your best friend. I know when something's wrong.'

I hesitate. I don't want Kimmy to be mad at me, but I can't tell her the truth either! At least not the *whole* truth . . .

'Dad's thinking of moving to Australia,' I say, fiddling anxiously with my pencil case.

'What?' Kimmy's eyes widen. 'When?'

'In two weeks,' I say miserably. 'And he wants me to go with him.'

'OMG! Lucy you can't!'

'Settle down, class!' Mr Hawkins says, striding into the room.

'Do you want to come over after school so we can talk properly?' Kimmy whispers. 'Hockey practice is cancelled.'

#Typical! The one day Kimmy can hang out I've got Operation Break-Up!

'I'm sorry.' I cringe. 'I can't.'

She sighs. 'Of course you can't.'

Great, now she's mad again. 'I'm sorry,' I hiss, desperate to get her back onside. 'I'm going to a spa,' I explain.

Her eyes narrow. 'A *spa*?'

'Ooh, which spa?' Nicole calls from across the table.

'Silence!' Mr Hawkins chides.

Crumpets! Now Kimmy's going to think I'm even more of a bimbo – especially as it's why I'm turning down spending time with her! I scribble a note:

It's not for fun – I'm going with Ingrid.
Dad's forcing me to spend some 'quality time' with her. It's gonna be a total drag!

I pass it to her.

I still feel bad not telling her the whole truth, but it's close enough. For now.

Kimmy frowns, then writes an answer, but before she can pass it back Mr Hawkins snatches it off her. They don't call him Hawkeye Hawkins for nothing.

'Let's see, what have we got here?' He peers at Kimmy's note, then reads it aloud in a silly high-pitched voice. '"Poor you – but don't you have detention today?" Well, unless you'd like detention too, Ms Chung, there'll be no more notes in my class. Understood?'

'Yes, Mr Hawkins,' Kimmy mumbles.

Detention? Oh crumpets, I forgot! Seriously, is amnesia infectious?

As soon as the bell rings for the end of school, I grab my bag and race into the corridor, hoping to get past Ms Banks's classroom without her noticing . . .

'Lucy Andrews!'

My heart sinks. There she is, holding her classroom door open for me expectantly.

'Where do you think you're going?'

'Ms Banks!' I cry. 'I'm really sorry, but I can't stay for detention – my mum really needs me.'

'Nice try, Lucy.' She raises an eyebrow. 'I spoke to your mother yesterday – she knows where you are.'

'But it's an emergency!' I protest.

'*Really?* And how did you find out about this emergency? Are you psychic?'

'Well, no, but—'

'Come on, Lucy, this isn't like you.'

'I'm sorry – can I please just nip to the loo first?' I beg.

She sighs. 'Be quick.'

I hurry into the toilets, dash into a cubicle and pull out my phone. Thank goodness for mobiles!

48 SHAZZA

I hate mobiles!

The loud sing-buzzing startled me, and now I've spilt oil all over the floor! Argh! I glance at the screen.

Lucy.

Uh-oh. I jab the answer button.

'Shazza! Uber-catastrophe! I completely forgot I'm in after-school detention today!' Lucy wails.

'Oh no!' I gasp. 'But I need you here! Now! To help me revise! You promised!'

'Ms Banks won't let me leave!' Lucy moans.

'Can't you sneak out!' I ask, looking desperately for a cloth to clean up the oil.

'I can't – the loos are opposite her classroom!'

'Well, let me talk to her,' I say, giving up and dabbing at the mess with my foot, hoping my sock will mop it up.

'We're not allowed mobile phones at school!' Lucy sighs. 'Shazza, you need to come and rescue me!'

'On my way!' I cry. I hang up, grab my bag – then slip over, landing hard on my bum. 'OUCH!'

I really hope the rest of the evening goes better than this!

49 LUCY

It's only when I hang up that I hear someone sniff in the next cubicle and realize I'm not alone.

'Who's there?' I call.

No answer.

I tap on the door. 'Come on, I know someone's in there. The door's locked.'

'Go away,' a familiar voice mumbles.

'Megan?' I say, surprised. 'Are you OK? What are you doing here?'

'Nothing. Leave me alone.' She sniffs again.

'Are you . . . crying?'

'No!' she snaps. 'I have hay fever, that's all.'

'In October?'

'Whatever. Tell anyone, you're dead. *And* I'll tell the teachers you brought a mobile phone to school.'

#Wow. Suddenly I don't feel so bad about the whole dress-wetting thing.

'Pardon me for caring!' I mutter, heading for the sinks.

'Lucy, wait – I'm sorry,' Megan says quickly. 'I won't tell, I promise. Is Shazza going to get you out of detention?'

'I hope so.'

'She's so cool. You're so lucky, Lucy. I wish my mum was like that.'

'What do you *mean*?' I spin around, stunned. '*Your* mum's *really* cool – she lets you wear what you want, buys you heaps of stuff and doesn't care if you stay out late!'

'Exactly,' she whispers. 'She doesn't *care*.'

'What?' I move closer, struggling to hear, to understand.

'I hardly ever even see her!' Megan moans. 'She's always off with her boyfriend.'

'Your mum has a *boyfriend*?' This is news to me!

'Who she's never bothered to introduce me to, by the way. It's like she's embarrassed about me or something.'

'Yeah, right!' I scoff, leaning against her cubicle door. 'Megan, you're beautiful and smart. Why on earth would she be embarrassed?'

'Because I make her look *old*,' she mumbles.

'*What?* That's crazy!'

'Come on, Lucy. She can't pretend to be young and cool if he discovers she has a teenage daughter, can she? Baggage much? Plus now she thinks I wet myself at your party. Even the Megababes are embarrassed to be around me, and I thought they were my friends.'

I cringe. 'Is that why you're hiding in the toilets?'

'It beats getting laughed at all the way home.'

My heart tumbles into my shoes.

'I didn't wet myself, you know.'

I know! I catch sight of my reflection in the grotty mirror above the sinks and I'm really glad Megan can't see me – guilt's written all over my flaming face. I feel horrible, like the scum around the plugholes. Worse.

'But it shouldn't matter if I had. Real friends would stand by me no matter what. Right?'

'Right,' I sigh, slumping against the door, feeling even more ashamed as I think of Kimmy dancing goofily at my party, and how I should've stood by her then.

'But real friends don't set you up.' Megan's voice hardens.

'What do you mean?' I ask, dread prickling down my spine.

'The Megababes were the only ones left alone with my school dress. One of them must've *wanted* me to be humiliated.'

'But . . . why?'

'I dunno.' Megan falters. 'Maybe they wanted me out of the Megababes? They'll have to change the name though!' She laughs bitterly. 'On Monday I was the most popular girl in our year; today I'm Megan-no-mates. Ironic, huh?'

I close my eyes – I can't even look at myself.

'Lucy! Are you OK?' Ms Banks calls, opening the door.

'Um, yes!' I scurry over to the sinks and turn on the taps. 'Just washing my hands.'

'Hurry up then.' She gives me a strange look as she leaves.

'You'd better go.' Megan sniffs.

'What about you?'

'I'll give it five more minutes. Just to make sure everyone's gone.' She takes a deep, trembling breath. 'And, Lucy? I'm really sorry about nicking your dress. You're a good friend. You're the only one I have left.'

I can't even bring myself to answer her. I scrub and scrub at my hands till they're pink and shiny – but no amount of soap can change how dirty I feel inside.

50 SHAZZA

By the time I get to the school I'm huffing and puffing –
Sharon is so unfit! - and there's only one other parent
waiting outside.

'Have you seen Megan? Megan Matthews?' the
woman calls anxiously as I approach. 'She hasn't come
out yet – unless I missed her somehow?'

'No, sorry,' I wheeze. 'Not since the pizza party!'

'Wait – you're *Lucy's* mum?'

'Right.' I nod, hurrying past.

'Oh, I'm so glad I bumped into you!' she cries, catching
my arm. 'I was just about to drop this round!' She hands
me a bag containing Lucy's dress. 'I can't tell you how
mortified I am about what happened.' She lowers her
voice. 'I can't believe Megan *wet herself*!'

'Oh . . .' I shift uneasily. 'It's fine, really.' I move to
leave, but she doesn't let go.

'It's never happened before!' Her voice cracks as she
rakes her fingers through her messy blonde hair. 'To be
honest I just . . . I don't know what to do with her any
more!'

OMGA! She's crying! I can't leave when she's *crying*,
can I? *What do I do?*

'Megan just hasn't been the same since her dad died,'
she sobs. 'She misbehaves, and pushes the boundaries

all the time. I-I've tried to cut her some slack, I really have — I've done everything I can to try to make up for not having her dad around — but she's clearly still really upset! Why else would she be wetting herself at her age?'

'Um . . .' My face grows hot, and for the first time I realize that my rad prank on Megan might actually have been pretty bogus.

'Unless she's found out about Kevin . . .' Megan's mum trails off.

'Kevin?' I echo.

'My boyfriend.' She sniffs. 'I haven't told Megan about him — I don't want to upset her when she's so fragile — but am I doing the right thing?' She wrings her hands fretfully. 'Should I tell her? Or should I break up with him? What do you think?'

'Umm . . .' I am so out of my depth!

'What would *you* do?' She gazes at me, her eyes tear-filled and desperate, and I panic. What would *I* do? I have no idea! I have no experience of parenting — that I remember, anyway!

But then I think of Lucy — of how she's always saying she wishes she could talk to Sharon like she talks to me, how she wishes Sharon had just confided in her, instead of bottling up her feelings and getting stressed out — and suddenly I know exactly what to say.

'Talk to Megan,' I advise. 'Tell her about Kevin, explain how you feel and talk everything through with her. Honesty's the best policy.'

After all, if Sharon had just been honest with Lucy, maybe she wouldn't have lost her memory. Maybe I wouldn't be here at all.

51 LUCY

Where's Shazza?

My eyes keep flicking to the clock and I cannot concentrate on the stupid play I've been given to read because my mind is torn between worrying about tonight and fretting about Megan – and it doesn't help that Nicole is sitting next to me, fidgeting and yawning every five seconds.

Suddenly the door bursts open.

'Sha— Mum!' I cry.

'*Mrs Andrews?*' Ms Banks's eyes widen. 'I almost didn't recognize you! What are you doing here?'

'I need Lucy!' Shazza cries. 'It's an emergency!'

'Told you!' I say, hurriedly gathering my things.

'Oh my goodness, what's happened?' Ms Banks jumps up. 'Is there anything I can do?'

'Oh no, it's . . . a parental thing,' Shazza says quickly. 'Nothing for you to worry about.'

A strange expression flickers across Ms Banks's face.

'Lucy's going to a spa,' Nicole pipes up.

I scowl at her. #Traitor!

'A *spa*?' Ms Banks frowns. '*That's* the emergency?'

'Um, well, yes . . .' Shazza falters. 'But—'

'I'm sorry, but I can't let Lucy out of detention for a *spa*.'

'It's not like that!' I protest. 'It's important!'

'Lucy, your education is far *more* important,' Ms Banks chides. 'You're supposed to be being punished, not rewarded.' She shakes her head and stares at Shazza. 'I must say, I'm very surprised that you would support this.'

'Obviously I wouldn't *normally*,' Shazza says hastily, 'but Lucy's right – it's really, really important. Trust me.'

Ms Banks's frown deepens. She looks really conflicted. 'All right. Lucy, you may go.'

Nicole's jaw drops.

'Thank you!' I beam. I knew she was my favourite teacher for a reason!

'But we'll reschedule the detention,' Ms Banks tells Shazza, lowering her voice. 'Rules are rules – I can't give Lucy special treatment.'

#AsIf!

'Of course!' Shazza beams. 'I owe you one!'

'Then maybe you could help chaperone at the ball on Saturday,' Ms Banks suggests quickly. 'Far more students are coming than we anticipated, so I've been roped into helping out, and we could really do with more parent chaperones.'

'Uh, yeah, OK.' Shazza shrugs. 'Count me in!'

'Great!' Ms Banks calls as we race out the door. 'See you on Saturday!'

52 SHAZZA

'Rad!' I grin at Lucy as we hurry home. 'I've never been to a ball before! How exciting!'

Lucy laughs. 'How ironic! The last conversation I had with Mum was her forbidding me to buy a ticket . . . Oh crumpets!' She smacks her forehead with her palm.

'What?'

'I still haven't got one! Can you remind me to take thirty quid to school tomorrow?'

'Sure — but we might need more cash after I bought all the ingredients for dinner.'

Lucy looks at me quizzically. '*Dinner?*'

'I'm cooking chicken cacciatore!' I declare, hooking my arm through Lucy's as we cross the road. 'I was so majorly nervous buying the red wine at the super-duper-market I almost dropped the bottle — I was so sure I was going to, like, get arrested or something — but they didn't even ask for ID! And I actually *had* some!'

'Do you know *how* to cook?' Lucy asks anxiously.

'Duh. You just follow the recipe, right? How hard can it be?'

Turns out, harder than I thought . . . For one thing, when we get back I discover I forgot to actually turn the oven on. Oops!

'Shazza!' Lucy cries in horror. 'Dad's going to be here soon!'

'It'll be fine!' I insist, twisting the dial. 'I'll just cook it for half the time at twice the temperature – sorted!'

'OK . . .' Lucy says, uncertainly. 'Now come on, we need to tidy this place, and you need to get changed – quickly!'

'Seriously?' Shazza pulls on the dark blue dress sprinkled with white flowers I've chosen, and cringes at her reflection. 'It's not very *me*.'

'You're not meant to look like *you*, you're meant to look like *Mum*,' I remind her. 'Besides, I remember her wearing it on their – your – tenth wedding anniversary, so hopefully it will bring back memories of a happier time. For Dad, I mean.' #Obvs

'Tenth wedding anniversary . . .' she frowns. 'Was that the one with the clumsy Italian waiter, or the one that Danny forgot?'

'Neither!' I cry, exasperated. 'It's the one where he threw you a surprise party!'

'Of course!' Shazza snaps her fingers. 'I totally knew that!'

OMG, Is this a mahoosive mistake? Perhaps I should call Dad and cancel . . .

The doorbell rings and Shazza and I stare at each other, horrified. #TooLate!

'They're here!' Shazza squeaks. 'Lucy, I can't do this!'

'You'll be fine.' I cross my fingers as I hug her. 'You've revised all the cards, you've cooked Dad's favourite dinner, now you just need to convince him not to move to Australia!'

'But what if I can't!' she panics. 'What if—'

'It doesn't matter,' I interrupt calmly. 'After what we've planned for Ingrid tonight, there's no *way* she'll want me as a stepdaughter!'

I feel her relax slightly. 'You really think it'll work?'

'Course!' I cross my fingers even tighter. The alternative is unthinkable!

The doorbell rings again.

This is it.

54 SHAZZA

'Hello, sweetheart,' Danny says as Lucy opens the front door. 'You ready to go?'

'I can't wait!' Lucy beams, winking at me as she climbs into the car with Ingrid.

I watch them drive away and suddenly I'm alone with Danny. Fear trickles down my spine — which is totally crazy. He's *Danny*. Like, one of my best friends — just . . . older. But I have never been so nervous in my entire life.

'Well . . . ?' He turns to me expectantly.

I blink. 'Well, what?'

'Can I come in?'

'Oh! Yes! Of course! Sorry!' I scurry backwards to let him past, then shut the door. *Awesome start, Shazza!* 'You look nice,' I say quickly, trying to make up for it as I hurry after him.

'What?' He looks up as he perches on the sofa — which luckily Lucy has cleared of pizza boxes! 'Oh. Thanks. You too.'

Awesome! Thank goodness Lucy chose my outfit!

'Oh, I've had this dress for, like, ages! Remember I wore it on our tenth wedding anniversary?'

He nods. 'How could I forget?'

'I still can't believe you threw me a surprise party!'

'I know.'

'I had absolutely no idea. You must've been secretly planning it for weeks!' I try to remember exactly what Lucy had told me. 'Then just . . . boom – SURPRISE! I was so shocked!'

'Sharon, I said I was sorry!' Danny jumps up, his eyes blazing. 'I've said it a million times. What more do you want?'

I flinch. 'What?' Holy guacamole, what's going on? Why is he apologizing? Why is he upset?

'Yes, I knew you hated surprises –' he runs his hands through his hair – 'but I thought you'd like the party! I *didn't know* you'd fallen out with your cousin and the last thing you wanted was to spend an evening with her – you didn't tell me!'

WOW. And Lucy didn't tell *me* that part. I guess she didn't know!

'But I get it.' He nods, gritting his teeth. 'You hate surprises. And I promised I'd never do anything like that again, and now I have, with Australia. Very symbolic.' He glares at my dress.

OMGA! *Stupid dress!* 'No, Danny, I—'

'But it's not the same, Sharon!' he protests. 'I haven't been "*secretly planning it for weeks*"! I called you the *moment* I found out about Ingrid's job offer, and—'

'DANNY!' I yell and he looks at me, his cheeks flushed. 'You've got it all wrong! I didn't mean anything by wearing this dress, I promise! I wasn't being symbolic! The last thing I want to do is fight with you!' Like, duh! I'm supposed to be making him hate *Ingrid* – not *me*!

I only hope Lucy's having more luck.

55 LUCY

The spa is amazing! As we step through the swooshing glass doors I am practically blinded by the gleaming marble floors.

'Welcome!' The kimono-wearing receptionist smiles as she checks us in. 'I see you've already booked your treatments online.'

Ingrid turns to me, surprised. 'Have we?'

I nod. 'I hope you don't mind – I wanted to make sure we could do everything together. They get very busy here,' I say, trying desperately to keep a straight face. Shazza and I had the *best* time choosing Ingrid's treatments last night!

'That's so sweet!' Ingrid beams as we head to the changing rooms. 'I'm so glad we're doing this, Luce.'

I grin. Not as glad as I am!

'Look, let's just sit down and chill out a bit, OK?' I suggest. 'Can I get you a coffee, Danny?' After all, apparently everyone loves coffee these days!

'Caffeine's the last thing I need.' Danny sighs, sinking on to the sofa. 'I'm sorry. I'm just a bit on edge, I suppose.' He rubs his brow. 'I knew tonight wouldn't be easy, and I know this is a really tough situation, and you must *hate* me for even *suggesting* taking Lucy away—'

'I don't hate you,' I interrupt, perching on a chair. 'I could never hate you, Detective Dan.'

His gaze softens. 'No one's called me that in years.'

I smile. Progress! 'Do you still have your grandad's magnifying glass?' I ask. 'You used to take it with you everywhere!'

A frown flickers over his face. 'No, don't you remember?'

Uh-oh. What don't I remember now?

'That year we made a snowman in the front garden and you decided he should be a detective – so you put my magnifying glass in his hand?'

'Oh yes, of course,' I lie.

'But in the morning the snowman had gone – and so had the magnifying glass.'

The smile drops from my face.

'Someone must've nicked it,' Danny continues, 'and

the snow melted, but Lucy was convinced he'd come to life and gone off to solve a mystery somewhere.'

I smile again . . . tentatively. So this is, like, a *happy* story . . . ?

'It's the reason Lucy loves snowmen so much.'

'Of course it is,' I babble, trying to cover my mistake. 'Not much snow in Australia though!' His face falls and my heart plummets. Me and my big mouth! 'I-I didn't mean—'

'I know what you meant.'

'No, Danny . . .'

Suddenly the smoke alarm goes off and I freeze.

Argh! The chicken!

57 LUCY

'Argh! Ow! *Ouch!*'

Wow, I can hear Ingrid's bones crunching from across the room.

#Excellent

I wish I could watch what's happening, too, but both our heads are tucked into those weird holes in the massage tables.

'OWW!'

Actually it's probably a good thing Ingrid can't see me – I can't keep a straight face!

'Are you all right, Ingrid?' I ask, biting my lip to keep from giggling.

'Uh, y-yeah. Oof! Are you?'

'Mm-hm. This is lovely, huh?' I murmur as my masseuse smothers warm oil gently over my back. I'm not sure which I'm enjoying more – my Swedish massage, or the sounds of Ingrid's uber-intensive deep-tissue massage. After all, just because we're having our treatments together, doesn't mean we have to have the *same* treatments . . . not that Ingrid needs to know that!

'OW!' she yelps. 'Ooh! Oh! OMIGOSH, that's great! I've had a knot there forever!'

Wait, what? She *likes* it? That was *not* the plan!

'Lucy – oof! – this massage is amazing!'

#Fail

178

Ugh. The chicken is totally burned.

I turn the oven off and swat at the smoke alarm with a towel, but it refuses to stop screeching, mocking me for my major uselessness. So much for impressing Danny with my cooking!

'Wow. What happened?' He walks in, reaches up and presses a button on the alarm and the noise stops instantly.

'I don't know!' I wail. 'Maybe the oven was too hot or I didn't set the timer properly . . .'

'Wait, you *burned dinner*?' His eyes twinkle. 'I thought it must've been a candle or something! I can't remember you *ever* burning food!'

Awesome. Now I've made him suspicious too!

'Lucy said you've been unwell,' he adds gently.

Yes! Great excuse!

'How are you feeling?'

'I'm . . . not quite myself,' I admit. 'But I should be back to normal soon.' *Fingers crossed!*

'Good. What was it, anyway?' he asks, peering at the charred remains.

'Chicken cacciatore.'

'My favourite?' His expression softens as he smiles. 'I think we both need to relax a bit. Maybe this'll help?'

He picks up the opened bottle of red wine left over from cooking.

Holy guacamole! I've never had wine before!

'And you know what goes perfectly with red?' He picks up a takeaway menu from the counter. 'Pizza. Ever since Lucy mentioned her pizza party, I have been *craving* it. What do you think?'

I grin. 'Genius.'

'Great!' He pulls out his mobile and dials the number. 'Hi, can I have one meat fiesta and . . .' He turns to me questioningly.

'Same.'

He looks surprised. 'You sure?'

I nod, then remember – too late – that I'm supposed to be a vegetarian. Oops!

'Make that a super-sized meat fiesta,' he says.

'But without any—'

'No olives.'

I smile. *He remembers!*

Danny hangs up, then tilts his head to one side. 'What happened to being vegetarian?'

'I . . . gave up,' I fib. 'Life's too short.'

'That deserves a toast!' He laughs.

'Sure . . .' I look around the kitchen anxiously. *If I was a wine glass, where would I live?* I open a random cupboard and find it full of tins. Oh fudge. The whole evening's like a major minefield!

Danny grabs two wine glasses from another cupboard and I blink, surprised – then remember he lived here for, like, more than a decade, while I've been here less than a week. Duh!

'What're you looking for?' he asks.

I scan the shelves in front of me desperately. 'Black pepper!' I grab it triumphantly and shut the door. 'Can't have pizza without black pepper!'

Danny laughs again and pours two large glasses of wine. 'To pizza . . . and second chances.' He raises his glass. 'Let's start this evening over again.'

I beam. That's *totally* worth drinking to!

'This treatment's really good for slowing the skin's ageing process,' Ingrid's beautician tells her. 'Close your eyes, please.'

'Great!' Ingrid beams, shutting her eyes obediently.

My eyes, on the other hand, are wide open. I don't want to miss a single second of what comes next. This is it – the moment I've been waiting for . . . Ingrid's facial. Her *snail* facial!

I couldn't believe it when I spotted it on the treatment list – who in their right mind would want *snails* on their *face*? Ugh!

I almost laugh out loud as the beautician picks up the first snail and places it on Ingrid's forehead.

Ingrid's brow crumples, but she doesn't open her eyes.

On goes the second . . .

Her cheek twitches, but still she doesn't look.

#OMG! How many will it take before she realizes?

Three . . .

Four . . .

Five . . .

The suspense is practically killing me!

Finally there are SIX slimy snails crawling over Ingrid's face! I SO wish Shazza was here to see! Just watching as they leave a slimy trail over her cheeks makes me shudder. Yuck! She's going to get such a horrible shock!

'Gosh, that feels really weird,' Ingrid says.

'Just relax,' her beautician says calmly. 'Try not to move too much – it disturbs them.'

'Disturbs who?' Ingrid mumbles.

'The snails.'

'The what?' Ingrid finally opens an eye.

This is it!

'Oh my *gosh*!' she gasps.

I grin, bracing myself for the bloodcurdling screams . . .

'I've always wanted to try this! Great choice, Lucy!' Ingrid cries.

Seriously? She's *always wanted* snails slithering over her face?

#Disgusting!

BLEURGH! I nearly choke on my wine – it is MAJORLY DISGUSTING!

'Are you *OK*?' Danny asks, patting my back. 'Did it go down the wrong way?'

'Mm-hmm,' I lie. How can grown-ups drink this stuff? I pretend to take tiny sips, then as soon as Danny goes to the loo I empty my glass down the kitchen sink. Gross! Now I need a replacement 'wine' so he doesn't pour me a refill! I look around and spot a bottle of blackcurrant squash. Perfect!

Quickly I pour it into my glass, then add water till it looks roughly the same colour as the wine.

'What're you doing?' Danny says suddenly, and I spin round.

'Just . . . getting a top-up,' I bluff. Will he notice the difference?

'Good idea.' He refills his own glass. 'I haven't had wine for ages.' He grins conspiratorially. 'Ingrid's super-strict about her diet – she has to be, really, being a personal trainer, but seriously – no carbs and no dairy equals no *taste*!'

I smile. Criticizing Ingrid is a majorly good sign. Finally this evening is going well!

61 LUCY

Tonight is not going well. At all.

'Ooh, that tingles.' Ingrid smiles as her beautician applies her face mask.

Seriously? Tingles? *Tingles?* It's a *bee-venom* mask – isn't it supposed to *sting?*

I close my eyes as my beautician slathers avocado goop over my face, glad I can't see Ingrid's irritating smile any more.

'We'll just leave you ladies to relax for a few minutes,' the beautician says, and I hear the door click as they leave.

Relax? I'm seething. All I've managed to achieve is to loosen Ingrid's muscles for the first time in years and give her facials that'll make her look even younger and *more* beautiful.

#UberFail!

'Ooh, Lucy, I can really feel my skin plumping up,' Ingrid giggles.

Terrific. Now her tiny wrinkles are being ironed out too.

'That'll be the bee venom,' I reply, hoping to creep her out. Unlikely, seeing as snails didn't seem to faze her, but I'm running out of ideas . . .

'Did you say *bee venom*?' Ingrid gasps.

My heart leaps. Maybe she's scared of bees?

'Uh-huh. Apparently Kate Middleton swears by it.'

Ingrid just swears. Loudly. '*Lucy!* I'm . . . allergic . . . to bee stings!' she wheezes.

'WHAT?' I yell.

I open my eyes – or try to, but the avocado goop is pretty heavy and I only manage to peek out from under one eyelid.

It's enough.

Ingrid's entire face has swollen to twice its size!

'Can't . . . breathe!' she gasps. 'Need Epi . . . Pen! Help!'

Then she passes out.

#OMG! I didn't mean to KILL her!

'Ingrid would kill me if she could see me now,' Danny grins, licking pizza sauce off his fingers. 'I feel like a naughty schoolboy!'

'Well, you were, once.' I smile, leaning across the table to grab another slice. 'Remember that time you glued all Mr Hammond's things to his desk?'

'I did not!'

'You totally did!'

'Why would I do such a thing?' he asks, holding his hands up, mock-offended.

I grin. 'Because I dared you to.'

Danny chuckles and swirls his wine. 'You were *such* a bad influence.'

'Er, you were just as bad!' I counter. 'Remember when you dared me to climb on to the roof of the maths classroom? *During* lessons?'

'Gosh, I'd forgotten all about that!' He claps a hand over his mouth. 'Didn't we get caught?'

I nod. 'Just as I'd got up there, Mrs Clark burst out of the classroom and found us.'

'That's right!' Danny gasps. 'I thought we were definitely going to get suspended!'

'Me too!' I giggle. 'But when you told her I was trying to rescue a cat she just went majorly gooey instead.'

'She was crazy about cats.' Danny laughs. 'I still can't believe she called the fire brigade.'

'*I* can't believe they spent a whole hour searching for a cat that didn't even *exist*!'

'Wow.' Danny wipes tears of laughter from his eyes. 'That feels like a lifetime ago!'

'It feels like last week to me.' Well, actually, it was . . .

'A lot's happened since then.'

'No kidding!' I snort. 'Who'd ever have guessed then that we'd end up getting *married*?'

'Or divorced,' he adds quietly.

My shoulders sag. 'And now . . . now you're moving to the other side of the world and I'll never see you again.' Tears prickle my eyes.

'Hey,' Danny says gently, passing me a napkin, 'this isn't like you. Where's the Sharon who always keeps it together? The Sharon who's always in control of her emotions?'

'I don't know,' I admit miserably, dabbing my eyes. *And I don't know if she's ever coming back.*

He sighs. 'Is this about Lucy? Because, you know, nothing's decided yet.'

'It's not just about Lucy, doofus.' I toss the scrunched-up napkin at him. 'It's about you too. I'll miss you.' I sniff. 'I miss you now.'

It's true. I miss twelve-year-old Danny so much it hurts. I miss all my friends and my family. I miss my life.

'I miss you too.'

I look up. 'You do?'

'Of course I do, *doofus*.' He throws the napkin back at me. 'You've been a huge part of my life for, well, a huge part of my life. It's weird not seeing you every day.'

I nod. 'Majorly weird.'

'I like the new hair by the way.' He grins. 'It suits you.'

'Thanks.' I smile.

'You look . . . younger.'

'I feel younger!' I laugh. Like, *thirty-odd years* younger!

'So . . . ?' He presses me. 'What's prompted this big change?'

'Umm . . .' I panic. WHAT DO I TELL HIM?

He winks. 'As if I didn't know!'

I freeze. Wait, he *knows*? Has he figured it out?! He was, like, *married* to Sharon for ages, so of course he's bound to notice I'm different! How did we *ever* think we could fool him? THIS WAS SUCH A BAD IDEA!

I feel my cheeks growing hot. 'Danny, I—'

'You're blushing!' He laughs. 'Don't worry – love makes us all act a little crazy, eh?'

My jaw drops. LOVE? Wait, does Danny think I – Sharon, I mean – still *loves* him?

Suddenly strange music fills the air. *What is happening?*

'Sorry.' Danny pulls his mobile from his pocket and his brow furrows. 'It's Lucy.'

Lucy?

'Sweetheart? Are you OK?' Danny stands up, suddenly agitated. 'Lucy, slow down. Which hospital?'

'Hospital?' I panic. Holy guacamole! What's happened?

'Stay calm, everything's going to be fine. We're on our way.' Danny turns to me, his face pale. 'Ingrid's collapsed.'

OMGA! What's Lucy *done*?

63 LUCY

What have I done? This is all my fault! I can't believe I nearly killed Ingrid! I can't believe I had to inject her with an EpiPen! I can't believe she's lying in a hospital bed because of me!

'Lucy!'

I turn to see Dad racing down the hospital corridor with Shazza.

'Dad!' I run into his arms. 'Thank goodness! She's in here.'

'Danny!' Ingrid wails as we all rush into the room. 'At last!'

'Ingrid!' Dad's eyes widen. The swelling's mostly gone down, but her face is still pretty puffy. 'Sweetheart, are you all right?'

'No, I – *Keep her away from me!*' Ingrid suddenly screams, pointing at me.

I freeze.

'What?' Dad blinks, then glances at me. 'Why?'

'Why? *Why?!*' Ingrid glares at him as if it's obvious. 'Danny, she's out to get me!'

Dad stares at her. 'Ingrid, sweetie, that's ridiculous!'

'No, it's not!' she screeches. 'Lucy obviously doesn't want you to move to Australia, so she's trying to get rid of me – she's been tormenting me all night! She booked all my treatments at the spa, and they were *horrible*!'

My jaw drops.

'First she booked me in for a really painful massage—'

'A massage?' Shazza snorts. 'How *terrible*.'

'You said you loved it!' I protest.

'Only because I didn't want you to feel bad!' Ingrid scowls. 'I did the same with the freaking snail facial!'

Dad's eyebrows shoot up. '*Snail* facial?'

Shazza winks and flashes me a thumbs-up.

'Exactly! Hideous, horrible, slithering slimy snails all over my freaking face!' Ingrid shudders. 'I can still feel them now!'

I bite my lip.

'And then – *then* –' she glares at me accusingly – 'she booked me in for a *bee-venom* facial!'

'But I didn't know about your allergy!' I insist, suddenly worrying that she might try to have me arrested for ATTEMPTED MURDER!

'Didn't you?' Ingrid narrows her eyes. 'Because it seems a pretty huge coincidence to me.'

'Dad, I didn't, I swear!' I protest.

'Of course you didn't. Ingrid, you can't possibly think Lucy wanted to *kill* you?' he cries. 'That's crazy!'

'Crazy?' Ingrid's eyes bulge. 'You're calling *me* crazy?'

'No, I just . . . I think you've had a shock and you might not be thinking clearly.' He kisses her forehead.

'Lucy's the one who saved you, after all!'

'Only after she – oh my God, have you been drinking?' Her nose wrinkles.

Dad steps backwards. 'Only a drop.'

'Danny, you *know* you're not meant to drink!' Ingrid shrieks.

Shazza and I exchange glances.

'How much have you had?'

'Holy guacamole! Only two glasses of wine!' Shazza rolls her eyes. 'He is a grown-up, you know? And it was with pizza, so that'll have soaked most of it up. Chill out, dude.'

'*Pizza?*' Ingrid gasps. 'You had pizza too? Danny, you know you're not allowed!'

Not allowed? OMG! As guilty as I feel for landing Ingrid in hospital, Dad is gonna be SO much better off without her. #ControlFreak

'Ingrid, calm down,' Dad soothes. 'It's no big deal.'

'*No big deal?*' she exclaims. 'You have a *heart problem*!'

'*What?*' I stare at him. 'Dad! Why didn't you tell me?'

'Because I didn't want you to worry, sweetheart,' he says. 'Besides, it's not serious. I just need to watch my cholesterol a bit, that's all.'

'Which is why I've been so careful with your meals!' Ingrid snaps. 'But what's the point, if as soon as my back's turned, you go drinking wine and eating *pizza*?'

Dad sighs. 'Ingrid, look—'

'Excuse me!' A nurse walks in. 'This is a hospital. There are sick people here. Please keep it down, or I'll have to ask you to leave.'

'I'm sorry. We'll be quieter,' Dad says.

'No. Leave!' Ingrid demands.

'Sweetheart—'

'Don't "*Sweetheart*" me!' She glares at him. 'I nearly died tonight because of *YOUR* daughter, and then you get here reeking of booze and tell me *I'm* crazy? I don't want you here. I don't want you at my flat when I get home. And . . . and I don't want you to come to Australia!'

'What?' Dad gasps. 'Ingrid!'

'Goodnight, Danny!' She turns away.

'No – Ingrid!'

'Sir, I'm sorry, you'll have to go,' the nurse says firmly, ushering us away. 'Give her some space, let her calm down. She's been through quite an ordeal.'

Dad hesitates, then reluctantly leaves with Shazza and me.

We did it.

We might've actually stopped Dad moving to Australia.

I look at Shazza . . . but neither of us is smiling.

64 SHAZZA

'Are you sure you're OK with Dad staying over?' Lucy asks as she climbs into bed.

'Course. After all, it's our fault he can't go back to Ingrid's flat,' I say, sinking on to the duvet miserably.

'I feel terrible,' Lucy groans. 'I mean, I know the whole point of Operation Break-Up was to split Dad and Ingrid up, but . . . I feel kinda sick now.'

'Me too.' I nod. 'I know she, like, broke up my marriage, but apart from that, Ingrid actually seems, well, OK.'

Lucy sighs. 'I always thought she was really bossy and controlling – I didn't realize she was just worried about Dad's health. I can't believe he didn't tell me about his heart problem.'

'I can't believe she pretended to *like* a snail facial!' I wince.

'I can't believe we *booked* her a snail facial! You should've seen it. It was horrible – all these actual live snails leaving slimy trails over her face!' Lucy buries her head in her pillow. 'I can't believe I landed her in *hospital!* I'm such a horrible person!'

'No, you're not,' I reply, stroking her back. 'You didn't know about her allergy.'

'No, but—'

'And everything you did was to help cure my amnesia,' I soothe. 'It's my fault really.'

'Shazza, it is SO not your fault.' Lucy sits up quickly. 'You didn't *choose* to get amnesia and you didn't *make* Dad want to move to Australia. I only hope it's worked. That tomorrow morning when you wake up, you'll have your memory back.'

I nod. 'I hope Danny's OK.'

There's a knock at the door and we both freeze.

'Sharon?' Danny calls. 'Could I possibly have another pillow?'

'Of course – I'll bring you one,' I call back.

I look at Lucy. 'Do you think he heard?' I hiss.

She cringes. 'I don't *think* so.'

I take a deep breath. 'Guess there's only one way to find out . . .' I grab a pillow and take it into the lounge, where Danny's spreading a blanket on the sofa.

'Thanks.' He smiles. 'And thanks for letting me stay over. One of the problems of moving into your girlfriend's flat, I suppose – when you argue, you have nowhere to sleep.'

I hug my arms. 'Do you think she meant it? About you not going to Australia?'

Danny slumps on to the sofa. 'It doesn't really matter. I can't go to Australia anyway.'

'What? Why not?'

'Look, I don't think for a minute that Lucy tried to kill Ingrid . . .'

'Of course not!'

'But booking her a snail facial?' He raises an eyebrow. 'That doesn't exactly bode well for a good stepmother–stepdaughter relationship, does it?'

I shift uncomfortably.

'If Lucy feels that strongly, if she's so determined to stop me going, then I just . . . shouldn't go.' Danny shrugs. 'She's my daughter. Family comes first.' He sighs heavily. 'I don't know what I was thinking. I can't move to the other side of the world. I can't make her choose between you and me. It's not fair.'

Wow. He's not going to Australia! I should be over the moon!

But as Danny rubs his forehead his wrinkles seem deeper than ever. He looks tired – and old. Older than I've ever seen him. And so sad.

'You really like her, don't you?' I say quietly, sitting down beside him.

'Yeah.' He sighs. 'I love her.'

My insides tighten painfully. Love? I've never heard Danny talk about love before, and it hurts. It hurts that he loves Ingrid, that she's not just a fling. But most of all it hurts to know that it's my fault they broke up – that he's so miserable – because of *me*.

197

I put my hand on his. 'I'm so sorry,' I whisper, my voice cracking.

'You're a strange one, Sharon,' Danny says, squeezing my hand. 'Any other ex would be cheering right now. You didn't want me to go to Australia, and you certainly didn't want Lucy to come with me. Now both those things are out the window, but you don't look happy about it.'

'I am glad you're not going,' I admit, 'but . . .'

'But what?'

'How could I possibly be happy when you're so sad?'

He pulls me into a hug I don't deserve and I feel like crying. All this time Lucy and I have been putting Sharon's happiness first, made getting her back our top priority, but what about Danny? Doesn't he deserve to be happy too?

'You're such a good friend,' he says. 'You always have been.'

I screw my eyes shut. If only he knew the truth!

'And you were right.'

'About what?'

'When you suggested we should separate. That we should just be friends.'

My eyes fly open. SHARON suggested the divorce?

'You know, I hadn't even really realized what had happened to us, but you were right. We were more like friends. *Best* friends, room-mates, but friends nonetheless.'

Is THAT what happened? It wasn't anything to do with Ingrid?

'But you're right, life's about so much more than that. We deserve to be truly happy.' He pulls back and smiles as he hooks his pinky round mine. 'Friends forever, right?'

Guilt swims in my stomach as I nod. 'Friends forever.'

But I feel like the worst friend in the world.

FRIDAY

65 LUCY

I wake to the smell of coffee and bacon and my eyes fly open. OMG, Mum's back! She must be! Shazza *hates* coffee! And Mum *always* cooks me bacon on special occasions! Dad and Ingrid breaking up must have cured her amnesia after all – thank goodness it wasn't all for nothing!

I jump out of bed and race to the kitchen to find Mum still in her nightie, sitting at the table. I have never been more thrilled to see her.

'Mum!' I fly at her in a hug.

'Watch it, Luce!' She laughs. 'You nearly sent my bacon and eggs flying!'

'Your . . . *bacon*?' #RedAlert

'You got a hug for your old dad too?'

I spin round to see him cooking at the hob, and my heart sinks.

Mum isn't back.

We broke Dad and Ingrid up for no reason.

'How many rashers would you like, sweetheart?'

'Just one, please,' I mumble, hugging Dad tight, my appetite gone.

'*One?* But I've got five ready!' he protests. 'I can't eat four rashers by myself!'

'Especially with your heart problem,' I remind him.

'I'll have some more!' Shazza jumps up.

Dad glances at the clock. 'Hadn't you better get ready for work?'

Uh-oh. Shazza's eyes widen in panic.

'Um . . . yeah . . . I'll go and do that.' She hurries into the corridor and beckons me to follow.

'What am I gonna do?' she hisses. 'I can't go to work!'

'Course not,' I say. 'You just have to make it look like you are. Get dressed in work clothes.'

'OK.' She nods. 'What are work clothes?'

66 SHAZZA

'OMGA! I look *terrible*!' I pluck in disgust at the frumpy skirt and blouse Lucy's picked out.

'I'm sorry, but none of your new trendy stuff would cut it as a librarian,' Lucy explains, pulling on her school jumper. 'You can change back once Dad's gone – we just have to keep up the charade while he's around.'

I shake my head. 'This is crazy!'

'I know,' Lucy sighs, slumping on to my bed, 'but we can't exactly kick him out – it's our fault he and Ingrid broke up!'

'And all for nothing.' I nod guiltily.

'Knock, knock!' Danny says, opening the bedroom door.

'*Danny!*' I shriek, bounding across the room and slamming it shut again. 'What's the point in saying "knock, knock" if you're gonna barge straight in? I'm getting dressed!'

'Sorry!' he cries. 'I won't look, I swear. I've just brought your mobile – it was ringing.'

'Oh. Um. Thank you.' I open the door slightly and he passes me the phone.

'It was Sam.' Danny smiles. 'How're things going? Have you told Lucy yet?'

I glance at Lucy, who shrugs and shakes her head.

'Um . . . no.'

'Look, I know you're worried she'll be upset, especially after how she's been with Ingrid, but she's a big girl, Shaz. She'll be pleased you've found love.'

My jaw drops.

'*What?*' Lucy squeals.

Danny's eyes widen in horror. 'Lucy's *in* there? Oh my gosh, Sharon, I'm so sorry!'

'Um – just give us a minute!' I slam the door in Danny's face and turn to Lucy, my mind majorly blown.

SHARON HAS A SECRET *BOYFRIEND*?

'OMG!' I hiss, jumping up. 'Mum's *dating* someone? In secret? *Who?*'

'How should *I* know?' Shazza protests. 'Do you know anyone called Sam?'

'Um . . . there's the guy at the corner shop. I think he might be called Sam – or is it Simon?'

'*Think!*'

'I'm trying!' I insist, pacing the room. 'But I don't know any of Mum's work colleagues. I've probably never even met the guy!'

'Well, let's just ask Danny – he obviously knows him.'

'Er, *no!* ' I cry, grabbing Shazza's arm as she heads for the door. 'That'd be well sus! – "Excuse me, ex-husband, but who exactly am I dating?"'

'True!' Shazza moans, drooping on to the bed.

'And Dad definitely won't tell *me* who Sam is if Mum hasn't,' I add. 'Especially after he just put his foot in it.'

'Argh!' Shazza flops backwards and scowls at the ceiling. 'But we have to find out who Sam is! He could be, like, the key to getting my memories back!'

I frown. 'You think Mum's secret relationship could be the real cause of her amnesia?'

'I don't know.' Shazza shrugs. 'Can you think of anything else it could be?'

I rack my brains but can't come up with anything.

'But why would Mum keep Sam a secret from me anyway?' I fold my arms. 'What did she think I'd do?'

Shazza looks up. 'How did you react when Danny told you about Ingrid?'

'I . . . threw a tantrum.' I wince. 'And ran away to Kimmy's house.' #Cringe. 'It's just – it's weird seeing your parents dating other people!' I sink down beside her. 'It's like . . . where does that leave me?'

Shazza props herself up on one elbow, frowning. 'What do you mean?'

'It's stupid, but when Mum and Dad were together, I felt I belonged, you know? But whenever I stayed with Dad and Ingrid . . . I always felt a bit like a spare part. A reminder of a failed marriage – the piece they can't get rid of.'

'Lucy!' Shazza sits up. 'No one wants to get rid of you!'

'But maybe they want to forget,' I whisper, hugging my knees. 'For a while anyway. Maybe *that's* why Mum kept her boyfriend secret. Maybe she kept me secret from him too? It's easier to start afresh without any baggage, right?'

Shazza stares at me. '*Baggage?*'

'That's what Megan says.' I shrug, my throat tight. 'She thinks her mum's too embarrassed to introduce her to her new boyfriend – what if Mum's the same?'

'Don't be ridiculous!' Shazza cries. 'Besides, Megan's mum isn't *embarrassed* about her! She was just worried about upsetting her. Megan's her top priority. And you're ours. Look at Danny – he's staying in England because you're the most important thing in his life.'

'And now his relationship has broken up because of me! You're *here* because of me! This is all my fault!' I sob, burying my head in my arms.

'No, it's not!' Shazza hugs me tight. 'None of it is.'

'You don't know that!' I protest. 'You don't know what our relationship was like before. Mum and I hardly spoke – not about important stuff. I couldn't tell her half the things I've told you, and – and she obviously couldn't talk to me either! If she had, maybe she wouldn't have lost her memory!'

'Oh, Lucy.' Shazza strokes my hair.

'I wish she'd told me,' I say with a sniff. 'Yes, I might've freaked out, yes, it would've been totally weird, but I'd have got used to it. If this guy – *Sam*, whoever he is – makes her happy, then . . . I'd be happy for her.'

'Then that's how we fix this!' Shazza cries, sitting up excitedly. 'You have to find Sam and give him your blessing! We just need to work out who he *is* – preferably before he calls again!'

#LightBulb

'Let's call *him* instead!' I cry, grabbing Mum's mobile. 'You've got his number right here – maybe I'll recognize his voice.'

'No way! I can't *talk* to him!' Shazza squeaks, leaping off the bed. 'He thinks I'm his *girlfriend*! I'd probably say something *majorly* wrong, ruin *everything* and then I'll *never* get my memory back – and it's not like I can introduce you to him over the phone *anyway*, so—'

'Shazza, calm down! You don't have to talk to him – I just need to hear his voice,' I explain. 'Hopefully we'll get his voicemail – if not, we'll just keep quiet and he'll think it's a pocket dial.'

'A what?'

'You know, that you've called him by accident – you've sat on your phone.'

'OK...' She sits back down nervously and I dial Sam's number, put the phone on loudspeaker and place it between us on the bed. Shazza twirls her hair nervously and my heart beats loudly as the phone rings. And rings.

Then suddenly it stops.

'Hello?' a woman's voice says.

Shazza and I stare at each other in shock, then we both lunge for the mobile to turn it off – and it tumbles to the floor. Behind the bed!

'Oh fudge!' Shazza cries. Out loud.

#Facepalm

'Hello?' the woman says again. 'Are you all right?'

I try reaching down the gap it fell down, but my arm's too big. I drop to the floor instead, and spot the phone –

but it's too far under. I search desperately for something to retrieve it with . . .

'Hello?' the woman says again. 'Can you hear me? Hello?'

Shazza tosses me a clothes hanger and I try again. Nearly . . . almost . . . Got it!

'*Hello?*'

I drag the mobile out from under the bed and quickly end the call.

'Phew!'

'Holy guacamole!' Shazza gasps, sinking to the floor beside me. '*Who* was *that*? Sam's *girlfriend*? Or . . . *wife*?' Her eyes widen with horror. 'Of course! *That's* why Sharon was keeping their relationship secret! No wonder she was majorly stressed out!'

'No way!' My head spins. 'I can't believe Mum would have an *affair*!'

'But . . . what other explanation is there?' Shazza frowns. 'Who else would be answering Sam's mobile this early in the morning? And why else would Sharon keep her relationship a secret from you?'

I bite my lip. I have no idea.

Suddenly her phone starts ringing and we both stare at the screen.

'Sam'.

'What should I do? What if it's Sam's wife calling back? What if it's *Sam himself*?' I recoil in horror as the phone buzzes angrily on the floor. 'I can't answer it!'

'No way!' Lucy agrees. She jabs at it and the ringing stops.

Phew!

Then the landline starts ringing. Lucy and I stare at each other.

'Oh fudge!' I squeak.

'It's OK,' Lucy soothes. 'No one knows you're home. We just won't answer it.'

We listen as it rings a few more times, then finally stops. I breathe a sigh of relief.

A knock on the bedroom door makes us both jump. We stare at each other fearfully. It can't be . . . *Can it?*

'Hello? Are you girls all right in there?'

Danny! I'd forgotten all about him!

'Um, yes, fine, thanks, Dad!' Lucy replies, shooting me a relieved smile.

'Only there's, um, a phone call for your mum. It's Sam.'

'Oh fudge!' I hiss. 'Danny answered it! What are we going to do?'

'Um . . . Mum can't come to the phone right now,' Lucy shouts.

'Why? What's wrong?' Danny sounds concerned. 'Is everything OK?'

'Everything's fine,' Lucy lies. 'Mum's just a bit . . . emotional. Can you say she's in the shower or something?'

'OK . . . Listen, I need to go to work now. But would it possibly be OK if I stay tonight too?' Danny calls.

'Of c-course,' I stutter, trying my best to sound 'emotional'.

Lucy rolls her eyes.

'Thanks, Shaz, I really appreciate it. Sorry for . . . everything.' He sighs. 'See you later.' His footsteps disappear down the hall.

Lucy shakes her head. 'Dad can't keep staying here, Shazza. It's too risky!'

'I know — but like you said, we can hardly kick him out,' I shrug helplessly.

'No.' Lucy takes a deep breath. 'We need to get Dad and Ingrid back together. We have to launch Operation Make-Up.'

I smile, suddenly feeling a huge rush of love for her.

'I hardly slept all night,' she moans, wringing her hands miserably. 'What we did was uber-wrong — especially as it hasn't brought your memory back anyway. Whether Dad goes to Australia or not should be his choice, just like he gave me the choice.'

'Oh, Lucy!' I hug her.

'Of course I want him to stay, of course I'd love it if you two got back together . . . but that's not up to me, is it?' She sighs. 'More than anything, I just really want you both to be happy.'

I squeeze her tighter, a lump in my throat. I guess this is what it feels like to be a proud mother.

Suddenly my mobile beeps.

It's a text.

> **Sam:** We need to talk.

Uh-oh.

'"*We need to talk*"?' Lucy winces. 'That's never good. Maybe it's because Dad answered the landline? Sam's jealous!'

'Holy guacamole!' I cry. 'And then I wouldn't speak to him!'

'Or . . . maybe his wife found out.' Lucy's face crumples – the same horrified expression she'd had when I suggested Sharon and Sam were having an affair.

'You know what?' I take Lucy's hand. 'Maybe it's for the best. Who wants to date a cheater, right? Perhaps we should just text Sam back to say it's over?' I'm sure that's what Lucy wants.

She hesitates. 'But then . . . you might never get your

memory back.' She frowns, biting her lip. 'And it's not like we really know what's going on with Sam – maybe he's really unhappily married? Maybe he's getting divorced too? Or maybe the woman was just a . . . lodger or . . . something?' She doesn't look convinced. After all, that wouldn't explain why Sharon hadn't told Lucy about him . . .

'Well, there's only one way to find out.' I take a deep breath. 'We have to meet Sam.'

'Really?' Lucy asks, wide-eyed. 'But you were so worried about even *talking* to him!'

'I am,' I say with a sigh. 'But you're right. It could be the only way to get my memory back.'

Lucy nods. 'I'll ask him to meet on Saturday at the bandstand in the middle of town.' Her fingers tap rapidly on the phone.

Moments later it beeps.

Sam: See you then.

69 LUCY

All morning, all I can think about is Sam and Ingrid – my potential new step-parents – *if* everything works out. At break I nip to the toilets and text Dad, asking him to drive me into town after school, and he agrees. #Result! I message Shazza quickly:

> **Lucy:** Operation Make-Up stage 1 complete!

But I still can't figure out who Sam is . . .

'Are you OK?' Kimmy asks, catching up with me as I head back to class. 'You seem miles away.'

'I'm fine – just got a lot on my mind.' #Understatement

'Of course you have.' Kimmy squeezes my arm. 'Any news about your Dad? Is he still moving to Australia?'

'I'm not sure,' I say, guilt weighing like a lump of lard in my gut. 'Dad and Ingrid broke up.'

'*What?*' Kimmy's eyes widen. 'Wow! What happened?'

'I can't really talk about it here,' I whisper, glancing around the busy corridor. The last thing I need is gossip. Plus it's not like I can tell her everything anyway.

'OK.' She nods. 'Well, why don't you come over to mine tonight? Mum's cooking one of her famous curries!'

My stomach rumbles. If only! How I'd love some great home cooking after all the junk food Shazza and I have eaten this week! 'I'm sorry, I can't.'

Kimmy's face falls. 'Seriously, Lucy? You moan about me not having time for you, but now you're the one who's always too busy!'

The guilty lump gets heavier.

'I'm sorry, Kimmy, really. But tonight's Operation Make-Up.'

She rolls her eyes. '*More* make-up? One makeover wasn't *enough*?'

'No – not *make-up*—'

'Hi, Lucy!' Nicole interrupts, looking up from the Megababes' table as we walk into Ms Banks's classroom. 'Which spa was it you went to last night?'

'Um, Eden Falls.'

'I'll make sure never to go there then!' She smirks. 'You look terrible!' Cara and Viv giggle.

'Wow. I can't believe I ever wanted to be friends with you guys!' I scowl at them. 'Megan was right – none of you know the meaning of the word.'

Nicole jumps up and strides towards me. '*What?*'

'Friends don't *ditch* each other!' I retort.

'We haven't *ditched* her!' Cara protests.

'As if!' adds Viv, looking hurt.

'What?' Now I'm totally confused.

Nicole sighs and perches on the edge of a desk. 'She thinks one of us set her up.'

'But we didn't!' Viv cries.

'Obvs!' Cara says with a shrug.

'Wait,' I say slowly. 'So you're *not* embarrassed to be seen with her?'

'As if!' Cara scoffs. 'Megan's our friend. At least, we thought she was.'

'But friends trust each other,' Viv says sadly. 'And she doesn't trust us. That's why *she's* avoiding *us.*'

'I can't believe she thinks one of us would betray her like that,' Nicole adds.

'How could she even *think* that?!' Cara exclaims.

Oh crumpets, here comes another big fat helping of guilt.

This is *all my fault*. I caused Mum's amnesia, I caused the rift between Dad and Ingrid, I'm keeping secrets from Kimmy, and now I've split up the Megababes.

I am a walking disaster zone.

But how can I tell them the truth? Who'd believe that it was actually Shazza who framed Megan? No one, that's who. They'd all think it was me. They'd all hate me.

#Dilemma

'I thought you had detention yesterday?' Kimmy asks as we sit at a table in the corner.

'I did.'

'Then how did you get to the spa?'

'Oh, Sh— my mum got me out of it.'

'Your mum got you out of detention? To go to a *spa*?' Kimmy raises an eyebrow. 'Maybe my dad *should* talk to her?'

'What?' My head snaps up. 'Why?'

'Well, I know I said before that her strange behaviour is probably just part of getting over the divorce – that'd explain her makeover, as well as all the gifts and stuff, even turning a blind eye to you bunking off school; classic overcompensation.'

'Exactly.' Wow, that sounds just like Megan's mum.

'But I know your mum, and she would never in a million years come *into school* to get you *out of detention* – especially for something as trivial as going to a *spa* – with *Ingrid*, of all people!' Kimmy shakes her head. 'That makes no sense. Maybe she's having a midlife crisis or something?'

'Shh!' I hiss. 'Of course she isn't!'

'You're not a psychiatrist, Luce,' she argues. 'Dad could just casually pop over for a chat – just to make sure she's OK.'

'Kimmy, *NO!*' I snap, panicking. I can't let her tell her dad that Shazza's having a breakdown! What if he reports her to social services? 'Just drop it, OK?'

'OK! No need to bite my head off!' Kimmy stares at me, stunned. 'Lucy, what's going on?'

I take a deep breath, trying to calm myself down.

'Look . . . it wasn't just a spa trip, OK?' I confess. 'It was part of a plan.'

She frowns. 'What plan?'

I hesitate, but I have no choice – I have to tell her. 'Sha— Mum and I were trying to split up Dad and Ingrid.'

Kimmy's eyes nearly pop out of her head. 'OMG! That explains *everything*!'

'Huh?'

'Quiet, please, class!' Ms Banks barks, her braids swinging wildly as she marches into the classroom. 'Turn to act 3 scene 2.'

'The makeover and the new clothes!' Kimmy continues excitedly. 'Your dad left your mum for a younger woman, so now she's *reinventing* herself as a younger woman!'

That's one way of looking at it!

'Operation *Make-Up*! I get it!' Kimmy hisses as we flick through our scripts. 'OMG, are your parents getting back together?'

'Lucy!'

I look up to find Ms Banks staring straight at us. 'See me at lunchtime, please.'

'But I wasn't even talking!' I protest.

'I didn't say you were,' she says tightly. 'But you need to make up that detention you missed yesterday. I'll see you at one o'clock.'

I groan.

'Rules are rules. I don't care if your dog ate it, your cat weed on it or your hamster shredded it, no homework equals automatic detention,' she declares. 'That goes for everyone! I want your homework on my desk at the end of the lesson. No exceptions.'

'Wow. Someone's in a bad mood,' Kimmy whispers.

I nod. And it's going to get even worse when she discovers I haven't done last night's homework either . . .

#UhOh

But then I smile. For Ms Banks has just given me the perfect way to reunite Megan and the Megababes – without implicating myself at all!

70 SHAZZA

> **Lucy:** Operation Make-Up stage 1 complete!

I smile as I read Lucy's text. Now it's my turn.

I dial the number quickly.

'Hello, Forever Fit, how can I help?' the receptionist chirps.

'Hi!' I say confidently. 'Can I speak to Ingrid, please?'

'Ingrid who?'

'Um . . .' OMGA! I don't know her last name! 'She's, like, a personal trainer?' I gabble. 'She's Australian.'

'Oh, *Ingrid*,' he says. 'Yes, she's just walked in. Who's calling please?'

'Shaz— Sharon Miller. No, *Andrews*!' Though if I'm divorced, maybe it *should* be Miller . . . Why are surnames so complicated?

'Right . . . Are you a member?'

'No.'

'A friend?'

'Not *exactly* . . .'

'Then . . . ?'

I take a deep breath. 'I'm her boyfriend's – well, *ex-boyfriend's*, I think – ex-wife.'

'Right . . .' he says slowly. 'I'll see if she's available.'

Weird. I thought she'd just walked in? I twirl

219

my hair round my finger as I wait.

'I'm sorry, Ingrid's busy right now,' the receptionist says finally.

'OK – I'll call back later.'

'Actually . . . she's busy all day.'

My heart sinks.

'Can I take a message?' he offers.

'No, thanks,' I sigh. After all, if Ingrid won't talk to me, there's no way she'll agree to *meet* me.

Operation Make-Up stage 2 has majorly failed!

As soon as Kimmy and I join a table at lunchtime I take a deep breath and stand on my chair – before I have a chance to chicken out.

'Excuse me!' I cry.

'What are you doing?' Kimmy gasps, but no one else even looks up.

'*Excuse me!* Hello-oo!' I yell, waving my arms in the air.

Still nothing!

The dinner hall is pretty noisy, with all the clatter of cutlery and crockery. Wait – that's it! I grab a glass and spoon and tap them together – I've seen this done at weddings – but it just makes the feeblest of tinkling noises and *still* no one looks up!

'EXCUSE ME!' I shout again, tapping the glass harder and harder till I'm bashing it violently. '*OI!*'

'Lucy Andrews! *What* are you doing?' Ms Banks's voice makes me jump, dropping the glass, which smashes loudly on the floor.

Now everyone looks up. And points. And laughs. #Typical

'Sorry!' I cringe, jumping down and starting to scoop up the pieces.

'Don't touch that!' Ms Banks cries, grabbing a broom

and striding over. 'Lucy, what were you *thinking*?'

'Um . . .' I look around at everyone staring at me and my cheeks burn. 'I was just trying to, er, get people's attention.'

Everyone laughs. Except Ms Banks, who frowns as she sweeps up the mess.

'Why? What's so important that you had to break school property?'

I take another deep breath. 'I just wanted to say that I know everyone thinks Megan wet herself at my party . . .'

People start giggling and looking at Megan, who instantly ducks her head.

'Lucy,' Ms Banks scolds, 'this isn't appropriate!'

'But I need to tell everyone that she didn't!' I protest. 'Megan didn't do it. It was my cat.'

Everyone looks at me. Even Megan finally looks up.

'And now Megan thinks the Megababes are too embarrassed to hang out with her now, but they're not; they think *she's* avoiding *them* because she doesn't trust them any more – but it's all just one big misunderstanding!'

Megan and the Megababes look at each other.

'Anything else?' Ms Banks asks pointedly.

'Nope.' I shake my head, lowering my voice. 'Except, um, sorry about the glass. And see you at one o'clock.'

I hand her the teaspoon and sit down quickly before she can give me another detention.

'*What* was *that*?' Kimmy whispers. 'You don't even have a cat!'

'*Shh!*' I hiss, looking round to check nobody heard.

'Hey, Lucy!'

I freeze. It's Zak!

He leans against my table. 'That was impressive.'

I gawp. 'Breaking a glass?'

'No!' He laughs. 'I mean, getting up there in front of everyone. Standing up for Megan. Especially after she was mean to you the other day, nearly breaking your phone and everything.'

I shrug, my heart racing. 'It was nothing.'

'No, it wasn't. It was cool,' he argues. 'You're cool.'

OMG! Zak thinks I'm cool. I am SO not cool.

'So . . . are you going to the Black and White Ball?' He grins, revealing those insane dimples again.

#Swoon

Luckily I'm sitting down.

'Um . . . maybe?' If I can still get a ticket! After everything that happened this morning, I forgot to bring the money! Duh!

'Cool.' He grins. 'Well, maybe see you there. Hopefully they'll play some decent music this year.'

'Right!' I beam, desperately trying not to squeal or

clap my hands with excitement – or do anything else uber-embarrassing!

'See ya.' He waves.

'See ya,' I echo.

I squeeze Kimmy's arm as he walks away. 'Did you hear that?' I squeak. 'Zak just asked me out!'

'No, he didn't.'

'What? Didn't you hear? He was right here and he just said—'

'He said, "Maybe see you there,"' Kimmy corrects. 'That is *not* asking you out.'

'What planet are you on? It totally is!'

Kimmy rolls her eyes. 'Whatever. Just don't get your hopes up, Lucy. He's a lot older than you.'

I bite my lip, remembering what Shazza said about Trev.

'Besides, you haven't even got a ticket yet, have you?'

'On it!' I pull my mobile out of my bag to text Shazza to bring the money. She still hasn't texted back from earlier. Weird.

'They're sold out,' a voice says. I turn to see Nicole standing behind me. 'I couldn't help overhearing you,' she says quietly. 'Freya tried to get one this morning, but they're all gone. Sorry, Luce.'

'Yeah, right.' I roll my eyes. Nasty Nicole is so NOT sorry.

'No, *really.*' She crouches next to the table to look me in the eye. 'I'm sorry you can't come to the ball. And I'm sorry I've been mean to you this week. I thought . . . we thought you were the one who set Megan up and ruined our friendship. We were wrong. Sorry.'

'Oh. Um. That's OK,' I mumble, feeling guilty all over again. Maybe she's not that nasty after all.

'Lucy Andrews, is that a mobile phone?' Ms Banks cries.

Oh fudgeballs, here comes yet *another* detention . . .

72 SHAZZA

'G'day!' I say in my best Aussie twang as the gym receptionist answers the phone again. 'Can I speak to my cousin Ingrid, please?'

'Of course!' he replies. 'Who's calling?'

'I'm her cousin.' Duh!

'Which one?' he asks pleasantly.

'Er . . . Kylie,' I reply, saying the first Australian name I think of.

'Just a minute.'

I cross my fingers tightly.

'Kylie?' Ingrid gasps suddenly. 'Strewth, how amazing to hear from ya!'

Yes! I punch the air. What a lucky guess!

'Especially as I don't have a cousin called Kylie,' Ingrid continues, and I freeze. 'Sharon, stop calling me.'

'Ingrid, please – I have to talk to you!' I beg – but the line's already dead.

Strewth.

I follow Ms Banks back to her classroom and slump down at a table.

'Lucy,' she sighs, closing the door, 'is everything all right at home?'

I freeze. 'What do you mean?'

'Well, after your family emergency yesterday – is everything resolved?'

'Um . . . kind of,' I mumble. 'It's a work in progress.'

She sits down next to me, her voice gentle. 'Lucy, what's going on? You're usually such a good student, but lately you've seemed . . . distracted. You were off school on Monday, you didn't hand in your homework on Wednesday, there was the "emergency" yesterday, the broken glass a few minutes ago, and you know mobile phones aren't allowed in school.'

Wow, she's really been paying attention!

'I know things have been a bit unstable with your parents lately. That can't be easy . . . ?'

I shake my head. #Understatement

She smiles sympathetically. 'Divorce is always difficult, especially when your parents move on to new relationships. I understand your dad moved out? That he's got a new girlfriend?'

Wow, teachers really know a lot. Do they just sit in

the staffroom and gossip about us?

'Not any more,' I mumble. 'They broke up.'

'Oh.' She seems surprised. 'That must be . . . unsettling for you.'

'It is.' I nod. 'And I had to rush to hospital last night because Ingrid collapsed, then I was up late because Dad stayed over, and with everything that's been going on I just . . . I didn't have a chance to do last night's homework either – sorry.' I wince, bracing myself for another detention.

'I see.' Ms Banks runs a hand across her forehead and sighs. 'Well, that's understandable. In light of everything you've told me, you may go.'

I look up, stunned. 'No detention?'

She shakes her head, her beaded braids clacking against each other like maracas. 'And you can have your phone back at the end of the day.'

'Thanks, Ms Banks!' I jump up and hurry to the door before she changes her mind.

'And Lucy?'

I groan inwardly, literally two steps from freedom.

'I'm always here if you want to talk,' she says kindly. 'All your teachers are.'

'Um, thanks.'

'And if you ever need an extension on your homework, or have other stuff going on, just tell me, OK?'

'OK,' I call as I hurry through the door.

Teachers are so weird. Why would she be uber-strict about detentions in class and then just let me off the hook? Not that I'm complaining. Hey, maybe it's because I got Megan and the Megababes back together. Maybe it's karma!

74 SHAZZA

I climb out of the taxi, take a deep breath and push through the glass doors of the gym.

'Hi.' I flash the receptionist my brightest smile. 'I'm looking for Ingrid.'

'Ingrid who?'

OMGA, not this again!

'*Sharon?*' an Australian voice says suddenly, and I spin around.

Ingrid narrows her eyes at me. 'You seriously don't give up, eh?'

'No, I don't.' I shake my head, suddenly full of nerves. 'I can't.'

After all, Operation Make-Up is depending on me!

75 LUCY

I check my phone as soon as Ms Banks returns it after school, but there's still no text from Shazza.

#Weird

I ring her as I hurry outside, but she doesn't answer.

#UberWeird

Suddenly Dad's car pulls up, so I pocket my phone and plaster on a smile, hoping against hope that everything's gone to plan – Operation Make-Up depends on it!

'Thanks for the lift, Dad,' I say, as we drive into town.

'No problem, sweetheart!' He smiles. 'I was surprised to get your text though – couldn't your mum drive you?'

'Um, no. She's busy.' I hope!

'Right.' He glances at me. 'Is everything OK with you two? I'm so sorry I put my foot in it this morning – I honestly didn't know you were there. It wasn't my place to tell you about Sam.'

'It's OK, Dad. I'm glad I know. So's Mum.'

'Really?' He looks surprised.

'*Really.*' I smile. I take a deep breath and launch into my Operation Make-Up speech: 'Dad, I'm really sorry about how I reacted when you got together with Ingrid. If she makes you happy, that's all that matters. You and Mum deserve to be happy.'

'Thank you, sweetheart.' Dad's eyes crinkle as he

231

smiles. 'So, you're really OK with your Mum dating Sam?'

'Yeah.' I shrug. 'I'm fine, and—'

'That's great,' he interrupts. 'I know your Mum was really nervous about telling you.'

#Understatement. So nervous she gave herself amnesia!

'And I understand why. It's got to be a bit weird for you, huh?'

'Well, yeah,' I admit. 'The thought of either of you dating anyone else is weird.'

'Well, yes, but especially Sam,' Dad presses.

Especially Sam? 'Um . . . why?'

Dad's face relaxes. '*Absolutely*. You're right. Why should it be weird? I'm really proud of you, Luce. I'm not sure I'd be as cool about it if I were you, especially given Sam's job.'

Sam's *job*? OMG, is he an *assassin* or something? A drug dealer? Please, please, not a *politician*! I gulp, my mind spinning. #WhoIsSam? *I have to know!*

'Dad—'

'Lucy,' he interrupts, peering through the windscreen as we park outside the restaurant, 'is that *Ingrid*?'

I gasp, torn between being relieved that Shazza managed to get Ingrid here – and panicking that I haven't had time to explain!

'Ingrid?' Danny cries, hurrying out of the car with Lucy. 'Sharon? What are you doing here?'

I freeze. Hasn't Lucy explained? I was going to text her to check everything had gone to plan, but I've left my mobile at home . . .

Ingrid's hands fly to her hips. 'You don't *know*?'

'Dad! Ingrid!' Lucy rushes between them. 'LISTEN! I owe you both an apology. And a confession.' She takes a deep breath. 'Ingrid, you were right, I was trying to break you guys up. I deliberately chose horrible spa treatments to try to make you hate me – but I truly had *no idea* you were allergic to bee stings! I honestly wasn't trying to kill you!'

'I know that.' Ingrid sighs. 'I'm sorry – I overreacted.'

'No, *I'm* sorry! *So* sorry,' Lucy gushes, taking her hand. 'You've always been so nice to me, and I've never really given you a chance. And then yesterday—'

'It's OK.' Ingrid smiles sadly. 'I get it. You didn't want to lose your Dad. Neither did I. He's one of a kind.'

Danny smiles sheepishly.

Lucy nods, her face crumpling. 'It's just . . . the thought of choosing between my parents – of living halfway round the world from one of you . . . it's *horrible*.'

Danny puts his arm around Lucy and squeezes her

tight. 'I should never have put you in that position,' he says softly.

'But it's not about me,' Lucy says, pulling away and standing up straight. 'It's about you two.' She takes Danny's hand. 'Daddy, I will *always* be your daughter. But if Ingrid goes to Australia without you, you might lose her forever. And I know she makes you happy. I know you love each other.'

Danny looks at Ingrid. Both of them have tears in their eyes. Even I'm welling up!

'Please don't break up because of me — I'd hate myself.' Lucy sniffs, placing Ingrid's hand in Danny's. 'So . . . I'm taking myself out of the equation. I'm staying in England with Mum —' Lucy smiles at me, then swallows hard — 'but you two should talk, so we've booked you a table on us. Have a drink, or some food — no high-cholesterol stuff though, Dad.'

Danny laughs, and Ingrid gives a watery smile.

'But whatever you decide, I'm cool with it,' Lucy promises. 'It's completely up to you.'

Danny kisses the top of her head. 'I love you.'

'I love you too,' she mutters huskily.

I blink away a tear.

I have never been more proud.

SATURDAY

77 LUCY

Not even the pouring rain can dampen my mood after Dad calls the next morning to say he's back with Ingrid . . . but he's staying in England! They're going to try long-distance! #Result

'I can't believe it!' Shazza squeals when I tell her the news. 'Everyone's happy! It's perfect!'

'I know!' I beam at her. 'Now we just have to fix *your* love life!'

She nods. 'And hopefully my memory at the same time!'

We get to the bandstand early, trembling with cold and nerves as we huddle behind a pillar, scanning every man who passes by.

'H-how will we know which one's Sam?' Shazza asks anxiously.

'We don't have to – he'll recognize you,' I reply. 'Then you can introduce me to him, and hopefully . . . bish bash bosh!'

Shazza looks at me. 'Bish bash bosh?'

'You know – it should cure your amnesia.'

#FingersCrossed

'Only if he turns up,' says Shazza fretfully, shivering as she peers around. The bandstand shelters us from the worst of the rain, luckily, but it's useless against the icy wind. 'What if he's changed his mind?'

'Chillax,' I soothe. 'We're early. He'll be here.' If he's not already – the bandstand is pretty crowded with people sheltering from the sudden downpour.

'Sharon?'

We both turn as a middle-aged man taps her shoulder. My eyes widen as I take in his flat cap, army jacket and grubby jeans. He is *so* not the kind of person I thought Mum would date!

'Blimey! I almost didn't recognize you!' He laughs, hugging her. 'I like your new hair!'

'Oh, um, th-thanks,' Shazza stutters shyly.

Phew! I was worried he'd hate it – he fell for old-Mum after all.

Shazza puts her arm around me. 'This is my d-daughter, Lucy.'

'Nice to meet you, Lucy.' Sam grins, shaking my hand. 'I've heard so much about you.'

So Mum *did* tell him about me! A warm feeling spreads through me despite the chilly weather. She *wasn't* embarrassed about me . . .

'Lovely to meet you too.' I smile nervously. *This is it*. I watch Shazza's face expectantly, half sad that she's leaving, half excited about getting Mum back, but she just shrugs at me.

It hasn't worked!

'We've missed you at work this week, Sharon,' Sam says. 'How are you feeling? You shouldn't be standing out here in the cold if you're under the weather.'

'You're right – why don't we all go for a coffee or something?' Shazza suggests.

'All right.' Sam smiles. 'Why not?'

'Great!' I grin, although inside I'm anxious. Meeting Sam was supposed to bring Mum's memory back . . .

Maybe I just need to get to know him better?

78 SHAZZA

Oh my giddy, giddy aunt, I am majorly confused! *Why haven't I got my memory back?* And how on earth did I end up dating the world's most *boring* man? He's been nattering non-stop for the last half an hour – about *taxidermy*! I thought that meant taxes – or taxis even – but no! It's, like, STUFFING DEAD ANIMALS! I mean, EWW! I thought Sharon was a *vegetarian*. I feel sick just listening to him.

'You're still looking a bit peaky, Sharon.' Sam frowns. 'What was it you had?'

'Oh, um . . .' I hesitate. I don't want to put my foot in it again!

'It was just a bug that was going round my school,' Lucy fibs quickly. 'All the kids had it. Do you have any kids yourself?' she asks Sam, changing the subject quickly.

Atta girl!

'Not yet!' Sam laughs, and my blood runs cold. OMGA! Does he want to have children with *Sharon*? But she's OLD!

'Next April it'll be a different story though.' He grins.

I freeze as Lucy stares at me. He can't mean . . . Does he mean . . . ?

HOLY GUACAMOLE! AM I PREGNANT?

79 LUCY

NO WAY! Shazza can't be pregnant. She's too OLD, surely? I mean, I know Mum's put on some weight recently, but . . . OMG! Is *that* what she was so stressed about telling me? Apart from the fact that the guy she's seeing is a complete weirdo!

Not that it's up to me, I remind myself, swallowing hard. It's Mum's choice who she dates. As long as he makes her happy . . .

'Congratulations,' I manage. 'Is it a boy or a girl?'

'Dunno yet.' He grins again. 'But I'd like a little girl – goodness knows her mum could use the help in the kitchen!'

Wow! That is offensive on SO many levels. Shazza looks like she's about to throw up. OMG – is it morning sickness?

'Just kidding!' Sam chortles. 'Tracy's a good cook really.'

I blink. 'Tracy?'

He nods. 'My wife.'

I stare at him, torn between relief that Shazza's not pregnant and horror that we were right – Sam *is* married. *That's* who answered his mobile. Tracy. His wife. His *pregnant* wife.

Shazza looks at me and I know we're thinking the

same thing: what is Mum *DOING* with this guy?

'I don't really mind if it's a boy,' Sam continues. 'After all, then we'd get to name him after me!'

'You could still name the baby after you if it's a girl!' I shrug. 'You know, short for Samantha.'

He snorts. 'Since when is Pete short for Samantha?'

My jaw drops.

OMG! *He's not Sam!*

'Holy guacamole, I have never been more relieved in my life!' I cry as Lucy and I race back to the bandstand.

'Me neither!' She laughs. 'No wonder you didn't get your memory back! But if he's not Sam, who *is*?'

We freeze our butts off in the bandstand for another thirty minutes. Eventually I sigh heavily. 'We must've missed him.'

'But I don't understand – why didn't he call when you weren't here at midday?' Lucy frowns. 'Is your phone on silent? Have you got a signal?'

I pull my mobile out, but the screen's dark and it won't turn on. 'It's broken!'

Lucy takes it, presses some buttons, then groans. 'No, it's just out of battery! Didn't you charge it last night?'

'Didn't I what?'

'Never mind . . .' She slumps on to the bench. 'We missed our chance.'

'There'll be other chances,' I soothe, sitting down beside her. 'We've got Sam's number after all. We can arrange another meeting.'

'I know,' she says. 'And actually . . . I'm kind of glad you didn't . . . you know.'

'Bish bash bosh?'

She nods. 'I mean, of course I want you to get your

memory back, but . . . I'm gonna miss you, Shazza. I'm not sure I'm ready to say goodbye yet.'

'Me neither.' I hook my arm through hers. 'Plus now we can go to the ball together!'

'I wish!' Lucy sighs. 'I told you – it's sold out!'

'Pah!' I wink. 'We're not gonna let a little thing like that stop us!'

'OMG, I have never had so much fun getting dressed!' I laugh as we dance around to cheesy eighties music, painting each other's nails and doing each other's make-up. Shazza is *amazing* with liquid eyeliner (though a bit OTT with the fluorescent eyeshadow), and I grin as she drowns her freshly curled afro in a cloud of hairspray. You can take the girl out of the eighties, but you can't take the eighties out of the girl!

Finally we stand side by side in front of the mirror – me in my beautiful new sparkly white dress and Shazza in her black jeans, lacy top and leather jacket – and beam at our reflections.

If this is one of our last nights together, we are definitely going to go out with a bang!

But as the taxi pulls up outside the school, my heart sinks – our night might be over before it's even begun!

'That's Hawkeye Hawkins taking the tickets,' I say with a groan. 'Nothing gets past him.'

Shazza shrugs. 'Then we'll just have to find another way in!'

I follow her round the back of the school, then freeze as she points to the tall brick wall surrounding the playground. 'Sorted!'

'No. Way!' I gasp.

'Do you wanna go to the ball or not?' Shazza grins, running up to it. 'Come on, just get on to my shoulders! It's easy!'

'OK . . .' I say nervously, climbing on.

Shazza wobbles as she stands up straight and my stomach lurches.

'This does not feel safe!'

'It's fine! Now just, like, grab the top of the wall.'

I squeal as we lunge towards the bricks, but somehow manage to get my arms over the top. 'Got it!' I cry, clinging on for dear life.

'Great! Now, GO!' Shazza cries, shoving my bum with both hands – and nearly launching me straight over the other side!

The other side.

I stare at the sheer drop in horror. '*How do I get down?*'

'Hang on, Lucy!' I call. 'I'll come round!'

'OK!' she whimpers. 'But hurry! I'm scared of heights!'

Honestly, didn't she get ANY of my genes? I race around to the front of the school. 'Chaperone coming through!' I cry, squeezing past the queue and into the building. The school hall looks beautiful, decorated with black and white balloons, streamers and fairy lights. But where's the playground?

'Mrs Andrews?' I turn to see Kimmy staring at me. 'What're you doing here?'

'Kimmy!' I beam. 'Which way's the playground?'

'The *playground*?' Kimmy frowns.

'Um yeah, I said I'd meet someone there and everything looks so different now it's decorated!' I bluff quickly. 'Could you show me? *Please!*'

'OK,' Kimmy says with a shrug, leading me through a maze of corridors to a set of glass double doors. Then her eyes widen. 'OMG! Is that Lucy?'

'Lucy!' Shazza sprints across the playground towards me – with Kimmy! 'Jump down! I'll catch you!'

#AsIf! What if she misses? It's an uber-long way down, and the playground is uber-concrete-y.

'Come on, Lucy!' Shazza urges. 'We need to get inside before someone sees us!'

Oh crumpets, she's right. I could get into heaps of trouble! I have to jump. Now.

'I'll count down!' Shazza cries. 'Three . . . two . . . one . . .'

'*Wait!*' Kimmy yells, dragging a crash mat behind her.

'Where'd you get that?' I gasp.

'PE shed.' She winks. 'Sometimes it's useful being a sports nerd.'

I grin.

'Come on, Lucy! JUMP!' Shazza cries.

I swallow hard, take a deep breath and . . . *Poof!* The crash mat sighs as I land on it.

I can't believe it!

I survived!

But my dress didn't.

'Lucy, come out!' Kimmy calls through the toilet door.

'Come on,' I urge. 'It can't be that bad.'

'*Can't it?*' Lucy cries. The cubicle door flies open and she storms out.

Holy guacamole! The rip is pretty huge. She ran into the toilets so quickly, this is the first time I've got a proper look. OMGA.

'See!' she wails. 'There's no way I can go out there with my bum on display! I'm gonna have to stay in here till everyone's gone.'

'Don't be silly – you'll miss the whole ball!' I protest.

'And you've been looking forward to it for ages,' Kimmy adds sadly.

'I know! I'll just nip home and get you something else to wear!' I offer.

'I don't *have* any other black or white dresses!' Lucy moans.

Suddenly there's a loud squeal. 'OMG, what *HAPPENED*?'

I turn to see Megan and the Barbie dolls staring at Lucy.

Oh fudge.

85 LUCY

I slam the cubicle door behind me and slump down on the toilet seat, trying not to cry. This is pants! Literally!

'Get lost, Megan,' Kimmy growls.

'Chillax, Chung,' Megan replies. 'Luce, are you OK? Come out.'

'As if!' So I can give the Megababes an opportunity to take photos and humiliate me in front of the whole school? I don't think so.

'Zak's been asking after you,' Megan adds.

#Crumpets. Zak. All this effort to get permission to come, to sneak in, for this one perfect night . . . all for nothing.

'Tell him . . . Tell him I couldn't make it,' I say with a sniff. 'I can't let Zak see me like this.'

'Seriously?' Megan says. 'OMG. If you're not coming out, I'm coming in.'

Huh?

Suddenly her head appears underneath the cubicle door.

'Megan!' I shriek. '*Get out!*'

'Uh-uh. I need to assess the damage.' She wriggles under the door, stands up, brushes off her black dress and looks me up and down. 'Right. Nicole, pass me your wrap. And Viv and Cara, I'll need your brooches.'

'What? Why?' I splutter, but moments later all three items are slid under the door.

'Now hold still . . .' Megan clips the brooches to my dress, holding it back together.

'There's still a big gap!' I whimper.

'I'm not finished.' She ties the glittery white wrap around my waist like a sarong and arranges the ends so they cascade like a waterfall. 'There. Sorted.'

'Really?' I say, peering at it doubtfully. 'Are you sure you can't see the split?'

'All I can see is a beautiful girl in a one-of-a-kind dress!' Megan smiles.

#Wow! Megan called me beautiful.

'Now come on.' She grins. 'Zak's waiting. Plus I'm really fed up of hiding in toilets!'

I take a deep breath, open the door and step outside.

'Oh, Lucy, it's perfect!' Shazza gasps.

I stare at my reflection, gobsmacked. Megan has done an amazing job. You can't see the rip at all, the brooches on the side are a great feature and the white sarong flows beautifully when I twirl. It looks even better than before!

Kimmy grins. 'Nice one, guys.'

'Thanks, Chung.' Megan beams and I smile. Maybe we can all be friends together after all.

'Come on!' Megan cries as we head to the dance floor. 'I've asked the DJ to play "Holiday" and we need to brush up on the moves!'

'Count me out — I don't know any of them!' Kimmy says, hanging back.

'Don't worry, we'll teach you!' Lucy smiles, taking her hand as she and the Megababes get into their starting positions. 'Is this right, Shazza?'

'Perfect!' I grin. I'm so thrilled they're all finally getting along!

'Sharon! You're here!' It's Megan's mum. She hurries over and hugs me. 'I wanted to thank you for your advice the other day.' She pulls me to one side, her eyes sparkling. 'I told Megan about my boyfriend, and they're actually getting on like a house on fire! You were so right. Honesty really is the best policy.'

'You're welcome!' I beam. 'I'm so happy for you!'

'Excuse me?' Someone taps me on the shoulder.

'Ms Banks!' I grin, turning to her. 'I'm here, just like I promised! I love your dress!' She looks amazing in her one-shouldered, floor-length white gown, her braids pinned up neatly with a white rose.

'Thanks,' she says, but doesn't smile. 'Could I have a word, please?'

'Um . . . of course.' I follow her into the corridor. Oh fudge — is Lucy in more trouble? Does she know we broke in?

OMGA, are we gonna get kicked out!

'Lucy?' a boy's voice says.

I turn. OMG! It's Zak! He looks amazing in his black shirt and trousers.

'Would you like to dance?' He smiles.

#Jawdrop

#Dimples

#Swoon

I nod helplessly, literally speechless.

Kimmy and the Megababes grin at me, and as Zak takes my hand a tingle suddenly shoots up my arm and my legs go all wobbly! This is incredible! I can't believe it! Zak asked me to dance!

I really hope my dress doesn't fall apart!

'I was worried I wasn't going to find you in time,' he says, leading me on to the dance floor.

'In time for what?' I ask, surprised I'm actually able to form words.

'I requested this song.' Zak smiles shyly. 'I thought you'd like it.'

I'm so giddy from being this close to him that I hadn't even realized the Star-Gazers are playing.

'I do!' I beam. 'They're my favourite band.'

'Mine too,' he says happily. 'They're playing a gig in town next month, and I was wondering if, maybe . . . you'd like to go?'

OMG, Zak's asking me out! He's actually asking me out! Woo-hoo!

Wait, *is* he?

'Um . . . like a date?' I check.

Zak shrugs. 'It's up to you. Bring some mates if you like? My dad's insisting on coming too.' He rolls his eyes as a bearded man wearing some old dad-band T-shirt waves at us, and I smile. Maybe I'm not the only one with embarrassing parents!

'I just thought we could hang out. I like you, Lucy.'

OMG, Zak *likes* me? Like, *likes* me likes me? OMG, there were too many *likes* in that sentence – I sound like Shazza!

'I like the way you don't try to fit in, or "be cool" – which is cool. Ironically.' Zak laughs. 'And I'd really like to get to know you a bit better. No pressure.'

I think of Trev. No pressure sounds great.

'That'd be . . . cool,' I mumble, my brain apparently giving up on making intelligent conversation.

He beams. 'Cool.'

I rest my head on his shoulder so he can't see the goofy grin splitting my face. I'd pinch myself to check I'm not dreaming – except if this is a dream I really, really don't want to wake up.

Ms Banks leads me into an empty classroom. 'Is it true?' she asks, closing the door.

I squirm. I SO don't want Lucy to get kicked out of the ball! 'Is what true?' I ask hesitantly.

'That you advised Megan's mum that "honesty's the best policy" when it comes to new relationships?'

'Oh!' This was SO not what I was expecting. 'Yeah. Why?'

'Then why don't you take your own advice?' Ms Banks snaps, suddenly looking upset. 'Why can't *you* just be honest?'

I blink. 'What?'

'Lucy's so confused, Sharon. And frankly so am I.' She sighs. 'Lucy says your husband's moved back in?'

'Well . . . yes,' I nod. 'He *did*, but—'

'So you *are* getting back together?'

'What? No!' I cry. 'He's back with Ingrid and I'm dating someone else now.'

'Someone *else*?' She stares at me. 'Who?'

I shift uncomfortably. I don't *know* who, but I can't exactly tell her that, can I? I fold my arms. 'I don't really think that's any of your business!'

Her jaw drops. 'None of my . . . wow. That's told me.'

Oh fudge. Was that really rude? She is Lucy's teacher

after all. 'I'm sorry if I've offended you . . . ?'

'Offended me?!' She laughs. 'Avoiding my calls was offensive, not meeting me when you'd arranged to was extremely rude, but dumping me for someone else without even bothering to tell me – then telling me it's *none of my business*? That really takes the biscuit.'

Wait. *What?*

'Would it have killed you to call? To text even? "Sam, I can't do this any more, it's over" – that's all it would've taken. I can't believe you've been cheating on me – and you have the nerve to tell Megan's mum that *honesty's the best policy*?'

HOLY GUACAMOLE! *She's Sam?!* It's as if an alarm has gone off in my head. Suddenly it all makes sense. Sharon's secret boyfriend is a *GIRLFRIEND*?

'All this time I thought you hadn't told Lucy about our relationship because you were worried about how she'd react, especially as I'm her teacher.' She sighs.

OMGA! So *that's* why Sharon was so stressed out! It all makes sense!

'But obviously the real reason was because you weren't that serious about me anyway! And now she never has to know, does she?' she continues bitterly. 'Well, I hope you're happy. Goodbye, Sharon.'

She walks out, leaving me literally speechless, my mind spinning in a million different directions. Wow, so

Sharon's in love with a woman? Future me is gay? Is that why it didn't work out with Trev? Or Danny? Or maybe I like men *and* women? This is so confusing – I have to talk to Lucy!

I hurry into the corridor, then stop myself.

Maybe I *shouldn't* tell Lucy . . . ? This must be what caused Sharon's amnesia after all. What if she was *right* to be nervous? I know Lucy said that being gay is no big deal these days, but will she feel the same about her own mum? What if Lucy reacts really badly and it ruins their relationship? And if it's over with Sam now anyway, why upset Lucy for no reason?

I twirl my hair anxiously.

But if I don't tell Lucy the truth, then I'll be stuck as a twelve-year-old in a middle-aged body forever and Lucy will never get her mum back . . .

What should I do?

89 LUCY

As Zak goes to get us drinks, Kimmy rushes up to me. 'OMG! I was SO WRONG about Zak!' she cries. 'Did he ask you out?'

I nod, and Kimmy squeals as she squeezes me tight.

'I still can't believe it!' I beam.

'Did everything work out with your parents too?' Kimmy asks. 'Did Operation Make-Up work? Is your Dad staying in England?'

'Er – no, yes, yes!' I laugh. 'He's back together with Ingrid, and Mum's got someone new!'

Kimmy's eyes widen. 'Since *yesterday*?'

'No, they've been dating in secret for a while apparently,' I say, looking around for Shazza, who seems to have disappeared.

'What a dark horse!' Kimmy gasps. 'I guess that explains her makeover! Who is he?'

'I still don't know!' I laugh. 'Have you seen her?' My eyes scan the crowded dance floor. I can't wait to tell her about Zak!

'Not since she went into the corridor with Ms Banks.'

'Ms Banks?' I say, surprised.

Kimmy nods. 'She didn't look happy.'

Oh no! Maybe she's discovered I'm here without a ticket!

I race into the corridor. 'Mum! Shazza!'

'Lucy!' Shazza rushes up to me, her face pale.

'Are you OK?' I ask. 'What did Ms Banks want?'

'Lucy, I . . . come with me. I think you should sit down.' She takes my hand and leads me into an empty classroom.

Uh-oh. This does not sound good. 'Am I in big trouble? Are we getting kicked out?'

'No . . .' Shazza smiles, but it doesn't reach her eyes. 'But . . . I've discovered who Sam is.'

#Wow! 'What? How?' I stare at her. 'Is Sam *here*?'

'Shh!' she hisses, closing the door behind us.

OMG. If Sam's here, that means he must be a parent, or a teacher or . . . or . . . oh please, no – not a sixth-former! I'd never live that down! No wonder Mum didn't want to tell me who she was dating! Maybe it was his *mother* who answered his mobile?

As soon as we're alone, Shazza hugs me tightly and I can feel her heart beating fast. She's so nervous! Of course she is. After all, Mum was so uber-stressed out about telling me about Sam that she got amnesia!

And suddenly I'm not nervous at all.

'Don't worry,' I tell Shazza. 'Whoever Sam is, it's cool.' I smile as I remember Zak's definition of cool. Maybe I am, after all. 'Shazza, I don't want you – or Mum – to ever be afraid to tell me anything. We're a team.'

I feel her relax in my arms. 'Thanks, Lucy. But before I tell you, I think we should, like, say goodbye. Just in case, you know . . .'

'Bish bash bosh,' I say quietly.

She nods. 'I'm gonna miss you so much.'

'Me too,' I say with a sniff, squeezing her tight. I feel as if my heart's breaking. I know it's silly. Shazza is Mum, and Mum is Shazza. But even so . . . this has been the most crazy, awesome, epic week EVER.

'Don't be sad,' Shazza says gently. 'After all, they say my form of amnesia can be recurrent – who knows, maybe Sharon'll have another major stress-out about something else some day and I'll be back!'

I laugh. 'I hope so! Well, not that Mum gets stressed out, of course, but . . .'

'I know what you mean,' she murmurs, stroking my hair.

I swallow hard. 'OK. I'm ready if you are.'

'OK.' Shazza nods. 'Lucy . . . Sam is –' she takes a deep breath and I can feel my heartbeat thrumming in my chest, my temples, everywhere – 'Ms Banks.'

MS BANKS?

Ms Banks, my ENGLISH TEACHER?

OMG! *THAT'S* why a woman answered Sam's phone! Sam = Samantha! Mum's in love with another *WOMAN*?

My teacher! Wow. I mean it might make it a bit awkward at school, but . . .

But none of that matters. Not if Mum's happy. Not if Mum's Mum.

A thousand questions fill my head, but they all pale in comparison to the most important one: *did it work?*

Slowly I pull back, searching her face for signs of a change. Is Mum still Shazza?

She blinks at me as if she's just woken up.

'Lucy?' she says tentatively, brushing a hair from my face. 'Pumpkin, are you OK? You look awfully pale—'

'*Mum!*' I throw my arms around her in a rush of love. 'Oh, Mum, I've missed you SO much! Are you all right? How are you feeling?' I pull back and she smiles.

'I'm fine. I feel better than fine actually.' She laughs and somehow she looks younger.

'Do you know where you are? I mean, what do you remember?'

'We're at your school ball,' she says. 'I remember everything, Lucy – it's like a dream. I remember having the best week of my life with you, feeling so young again, hanging out, dancing, talking about *everything*, and . . . and getting into several scrapes!'

I grin, tears prickling at my eyes.

'And I remember that I've just told you that I'm dating Sam – Ms Banks . . . and you haven't said anything back,' she says, beginning to look nervous again. 'Oh dear, I didn't want to spring it on you like this! I'd planned a lovely dinner together, just you and me, and I was going to tell you then, talk everything through before you had to make a decision about going to Australia, and then if it went well Sam was going to—'

'Mum, I think it's great!' I interrupt, hugging her quickly. I don't want her slipping away again! So *that* must have been the real reason she didn't want me to come to the ball . . .

'Oh, Lucy, I'm so glad! So *relieved*!' She squeezes me tight. 'You're really OK with it?'

'Mum, I'm more than OK!' I insist. 'If she makes you happy, I think it's absolutely awesome.'

'She does.' Mum smiles. 'She's amazing.'

'Then that's all that matters.' I beam. 'Now let's go and tell her!' I jump up.

'Oh gosh, first I have to fix my hair – and my make-up!' Mum says, catching sight of her reflection in the classroom window. 'And what am I wearing? What was I *thinking*?'

'Come on!' I urge. 'None of that matters. Just be you.'

Ms Banks isn't hard to find. She's slumped on a chair in the corner of the hall, looking uber-miserable.

'Hi, Ms Banks!' I cry, racing up to her. 'Or should I say "Sam"?'

She looks up and frowns. 'Lucy, I don't think that's appropriate.'

'Really?' I smile. 'Because I think we should be on first-name terms – since you're dating my mum and everything.'

Her eyes widen as Mum steps forward.

'You told her?' she whispers.

Mum nods.

'But what about your new relationship?'

Mum shakes her head as she sits down next to her. 'There isn't anyone else. I just . . . I thought we should break up because I didn't want to risk upsetting Lucy, and I thought it would be easier if you thought I was a horrible person . . . Then you could just hate me and get on with your life.'

Wow – even present-day Mum is good at blagging her way out of tricky situations! I'm gonna have to get some tips!

Ms Banks swallows. 'So that's why you've been avoiding my calls?'

'I'm so sorry, Sam, for the way I've treated you this week –' Mum takes her hand – 'but the thought of life without you makes me so miserable. You're right. I do need to be honest with myself – with everyone. I want to be with you, Samantha Banks. And I don't care who knows it.'

'OMG!' Megan squeals, appearing beside me with Kimmy. 'Your mum and Ms Banks?! No way!'

Wow, that didn't take long!

'I guess the secret's out!' Kimmy grins at me.

A shy smile spreads across Ms Banks's face. 'I guess so!'

'About time too.' Mum grins, pulling Ms Banks to her feet. 'Fancy a dance?'

'I'd be delighted.' Ms Banks beams, following her on to the dance floor. A fast song comes on and as they twist and spin around the room, loads of people stare and whisper and point, but Mum and Ms Banks don't seem to notice. Or care.

And neither do I.

Yes, it is hot gossip. And yes, English lessons are gonna be kinda weird from now on. But as I watch them laughing and gazing at each other like they're the only two people in the entire world, none of that matters. They look so happy. And so am I.

Then a familiar tune starts playing.

'*Luceee!*' Megan squeals, grabbing my arm. 'Come on! It's "Holiday"!'

Zak raises an eyebrow as she drags me past him on to the dance floor. Oh crumpets, there goes my cool image!

'Ready?' Megan beams at us as the Megababes – and

pretty much everyone who came to my party – get into their starting positions.

'Wait,' I cry. 'Where's Kimmy?'

'Behind you,' Kimmy says, and I spin round, delighted. 'You're joining in?'

'Maybe Madonna's not that lame –' she shrugs – 'and perhaps the Megababes aren't so bad either. Go ahead – say, "I told you so!"'

But instead I throw my arms around my best friend. 'You're awesome!'

Kimmy laughs. 'You haven't seen my dance moves yet!'

As the song begins we all move in sync and a crowd gathers around us, watching and clapping along to the rhythm. Normally I'd be mortified to be the centre of attention like this – especially with my Mum and Ms Banks dancing along with all my friends – but tonight it's the best feeling in the world.

Then I notice Kimmy falling behind with the moves. Finally she gives up, shrugs and smiles at me as she turns to walk away.

'Oh no, you don't!' I grab her arm. She is *not* sitting this one out.

'But I don't know the steps!' she protests.

'You don't have to!' I grin, waving my arms around madly. 'Just be as goofy as possible!' She stares at me, then bursts out laughing and joins in as we try to outdo each other with our silly dancing. Before I know it, the Megababes are busting some crazy moves too – and even Zak joins in! I laugh as he attempts the robot – badly! Who knew he was such a doofus? It makes me like him even more.

Mum smiles at me and mouths, 'OK?'

I beam and give her a thumbs-up. Everything's OK. Very OK. How could it not be? Dad's not moving to Australia but still gets to be with Ingrid, Kimmy's friends with me *and* the Megababes, Zak's asked me out, and Shazza's finally back to being Mum – for now anyway!

ACKNOWLEDGEMENTS

Enormous thanks . . .

To my wonderful editor, Rachel Kellehar, who is such a joy to work with.

To the lovely Venetia Gosling, for believing in me from the very beginning.

To my brilliant agent, Jenny Savill, and all at the amazing Andrew Nurnberg Associates.

To Naomi Jacobs, whose incredible real-life account of her amnesia, *Forgotten Girl*, provided a valuable resource when researching this condition.

To all my Facebook friends, for their companionship, humour and rapid answers to an array of random questions.

To all my awesome author friends, especially in SCBWI and The Edge, for their encouragement, comradery, advice and insights.

To the fabulous Jo Nadin, Jo Cotterill and Tamsyn Murray, for writing such wonderful books and for their generous feedback on *Mumnesia*!

To Push-In Boots, for always keeping me company on the sofa.

To Chris, for his constant love and support, for making me giggle and keeping me sane, and for putting up with me always getting up later than him and becoming a complete hermit when deadlines are looming.

And finally to my incredible family, who are an endless – and much treasured – source of love, laughter, hugs and inspiration. I don't know what I'd do without you.

Thank you all, from the bottom of my heart. x